THE DARTMOOR HORROR

by

Joe DeSantis

First published by Dog Ear Publishing
4010 W. 86th Street, Ste H
Indianapolis, IN 46268
www.dogearpublishing.net

ISBN: 978-1-4575-3415-7

This book is printed on acid-free paper.
Printed in the United States of America

This novel is a mystery, so it's fitting that the dedication should be likewise.

For S. M.

TABLE OF CONTENTS

CHAPTER 1

Unfinished Business

The carriage ambled slowly and deliberately over the winding country road, leaving a long, low cloud of dust behind as it made its way into the outskirts of the town. The driver, briefly energized by the appearance of the scattered, outlying cottages, gave his whip a sharp snap onto the rump of the solitary old horse pulling its burden along.

There was no noticeable increase in speed, as though the horse had decided many years ago to ignore such foolishness. The driver sighed in resignation and sheepishly placed the whip back into its holder.

While the beast had obviously seen better days, the carriage on the other hand was a truly handsome piece of transportation. Jet black it was, sparkling as though recently polished to a fine glimmer, while the large, spoke wheels beneath it were of a soft brown luster that gave off a feeling of warmth and security.

This was a conveyance not often seen in these parts without good reason. As it passed by the first set of simple, white washed thatched houses, a little girl in a worn, faded blue frocked dress stopped picking flowers along her front walkway and waved excitedly. The driver smiled in appreciation and tipped his hat to the pretty, young urchin, who ran inside with a squeal to report what had just happened.

Inside the carriage, an impeccably well-dressed squire stared absent mindedly out the open window while the curtains swayed back and forth with the forward motion. He did not feel the fresh air on his cheeks, nor did he appear to recognize his surroundings. His mind was far away, and his brow was furrowed, as though lost in a melancholy dream from which he could not hope to awaken.

Finally, once in the center of town, such as it was, the carriage pulled up to a nondescript two story structure that had an obvious institutional look to it. The driver hopped down and glanced quickly at the large wooden sign over the front doorway. The black print read:

Grimpen Post Office & Gaol

Townsfolk were bustling in and out with letters and assorted packages, but when they glanced at the carriage, all stopped in their tracks and whispered amongst themselves in a near reverence most often reserved for Sunday service.

The driver stepped back and stood ram rod straight by the carriage door, his hand reaching purposefully for the outside handle. This was a pose he had assumed many times in the past. He then opened the door with a slight jerk, and as he did so, the family coat of arms placed on it came towards him in a rush.

Painted over a white shield was a red chevron whose bars began at the bottom corners and met directly at mid-point. Above the chevron on either side were two round blue disks, while a third disk was situated directly under the chevron. Taken in order, the colors represented sincerity, loyalty, and strength. Under the shield was a fluttering strip of parchment with a strange, three word Latin inscription.

But the most striking aspect was the peculiar image of a snarling hound's head above the shield. Within its jaws was a snapped wooden spear tinged with blood at the tip of the sharp metal head. The animal was in profile, with its ears pointed straight up as though on guard, and it's eye staring menacingly out to all who gazed upon its features. To the uninformed, it was a rare sight indeed, but to the everyday residents of Dartmoor, the beast's countenance made perfect sense. They knew the passenger in the carriage.

The coach driver stood expectantly by the open door with his shoulders thrown back, waiting for his passenger to emerge. Even the old horse turned its head with curiosity at the delay in the proceedings. After several seconds that must have felt extraordinarily painful, the servant cleared his throat and reluctantly spoke up.

"Ah…we have arrived at the Grimpen…Gaol, sir."

A voice echoed from within the carriage with a tone that seemed pained and distracted.

"Ohhh, so we have. Why, thank you Perkins. My mind…must have…wandered for a moment; so silly of me."

A handsome young man in a brown tweed suit replete with matching vest slowly made his way out, his feet simultaneously touching down in a final dismount from the collapsible step onto terra firma. It was an odd exit for a knight, but this one had a valid excuse, as he had been raised in the United States, and as such had learned to shy away from much of the stiff custom and formality of English royalty.

The square jawed squire stared straight ahead as he walked along the path into the building, ignoring the polite acknowledgments of the townsfolk who passed him on the way. However, they were not insulted by the seemingly intended snub. They sensed his pain, and appeared to understand the purpose of his visit.

He opened the weather beaten wooden door to a low sounding creak and stepped inside. To his left was the counter space for the Grimpen post office. A white haired old man with the obviously dull look of a career civil servant stood behind it waiting on a customer. A cubby holed bureau filled with letters was flush up against the wall further back.

To the right, a barrel chested constable with sergeant's stripes sat behind a large oak desk that had also seen better days. Papers were scattered in disarray all about it, and the man appeared to be searching in vain for a particular piece of official correspondence. He glanced up at the figure standing patiently before him; as his mouth dropped, his face quickly betrayed a look of complete surprise.

"Why, it's Sir Henry Baskerville, is it not, sir?"

The gentleman smiled and nodded his head slowly in agreement. "Yes sergeant, thank you. I was wondering if I might have a moment to visit with one of your…prisoners."

The constable hid his amusement at the question laid before him.

"This is Grimpen, Sir Henry. We have but one prisoner, and now that the convict Selden is dead, I am confident that it shall remain that way."

"I understand your meaning, constable. Nevertheless, I repeat my request."

The sergeant suddenly grasped the meaning placed before him, and as his face became flush with embarrassment, he stood up and gestured sharply at a door behind him.

"Of course, Sir Henry. Absolutely! Right this way, if you please sir."

With the constable leading the way, the two men entered the rear of the building. Oddly enough, they passed the lone gaol cell, which was conspicuously empty. Henry stopped in his tracks and stared incredulously at the unoccupied space.

"Excuse me, sergeant. Did you not say that you had a prisoner in your custody at this time?"

The man's official demeanor softened and he replied sheepishly, as though his position had placed him in an uncomfortable situation.

"Well...I do, Sir Henry, indeed I do. I just felt that...under the circumstances and all, I didn't see the need to subject the lady to such a grim setting, with no privacy per se. After all, she DID give me her word that she would make no attempt to escape, and that was good enough for me, sir."

Baskerville smiled and nodded at the constable in a show of appreciation.

"Thank you, sergeant. That WAS most thoughtful of you. I understand."

The constable blushed yet again and they continued to a door at the end of the corridor. He knocked gently and raised his voice so it could be heard inside.

"Excuse me; you have a visitor here to see you. May we come in?"

After a short pause, a soft voice replied with a tinge of consternation in her voice.

"A visitor...for ME? Why, of course, by all means, please come in."

The door swung open and the constable gestured for Baskerville to step inside. As the squire did so, he took a quick glance around the room. It was sparse by Victorian standards; a bed sans headboard propped parallel against a corner wall, a small writing desk situated in front of the only window in the room, with an unlit hurricane lamp and some books piled high upon it, and a vacant cane chair behind.

Along the side wall to the right of the open door was a dressing bureau. In front of that bureau stood the most beautiful woman Baskerville had ever seen. It did not matter to him that her face was sad and drawn. At a time not long ago, to him she was the embodiment of womanhood, this person standing there in a simple peach colored dress, her arms at her side. The constable broke the long, uncomfortable silence.

"Well now…I recollect that I have some paperwork to catch up on, IF I can find it, that is, so I shall leave the two of you for some privacy. When you have done with your visit, sir, just come up to the front desk and I can let you out."

With his introductory speech over, the constable happily made a swift exit. The two stood staring at each other intently, until the woman broke the tension in a quivering voice filled with shame and regret.

"Oh, Henry, why did you come? You are only making things worse, can't you see that?"

"I just wanted to hear the story from your own lips, Beryl. Mr. Holmes gave me the details before his return to London with Dr. Watson, but it's not enough. I need YOU to tell me the particulars, if only for my own peace of mind, so I can put an end to this ghastly business once and for all."

She turned, walked slowly to the window and looked outside, as though unable to look him in the eye, while she wrung her hands together in front of her like some biblical Pontius Pilate overcome with guilt.

"I doubt that I could tell you anything more than Mr. Holmes already has. My name is…or was, Beryl Garcia. I met Jack, I mean Rodger, while he was travelling in Costa Rica. I fell madly in love and married him soon afterwards without a thought of how he would provide for me. Little did I realize that he was an utter scoundrel of the worst sort; and yet, I stayed with him nevertheless."

She stopped for a moment and shook her head from side to side as though in disbelief at what she was recounting. Unfortunately for them both, it was all too true.

"He absconded with some funds, and we were forced to leave my native South America; but I did not care, because I was still with HIM, you understand. We came to England and he took the name Vandeleur in an effort to keep the police off our trail.

Rodger took over a boys' school in Yorkshire, but even though the police could not find us, bad luck most certainly did. An epidemic within the school cost several lives, forcing us to move yet again, and he changed his name to Jack Stapleton; but this time we made for Dartmoor, where he knew his prosperous ancestors still dwelled."

It was now that Beryl turned around to face Henry. It was the least she could do for him at this stage of the "game," as the Great Detective was so fond of saying.

"He bought nearby Merripit House to keep a close eye on Sir Charles at Baskerville Hall, and took on the appearance of a naturalist, which was not a difficult task, since he in fact was one in his heart. It was at this time that he learned of the family's legendary hound, and he concocted the vile scheme eventually uncovered by Mr. Holmes to steal away the family inheritance."

It was then that the squire raised his hand in the air and interrupted.

"A scheme that YOU YOURSELF had knowledge of yet did nothing to stop while your husband murdered my poor uncle in the foulest way, is that not so?"

"I cannot and will not deny it, Henry, but I refused to take part in YOUR murder. Do not the rope burns on my wrists attest to my statement?"

Beryl held them out palms up anxiously to him for validation, but he would not look upon them. She lowered her head and finished her story.

"Well...there is not much left to tell, is there, Henry? The hound has been shot dead by Mr. Holmes, My husband has been swallowed up in the Grimpen Mire, and you are safe and sound once more."

He then looked at her with such intensity that she turned away in humiliation, for she knew what he would ask next.

"But what of US, Beryl? Was it all a lie? Have you no feelings for me whatsoever? I must know here and now."

Her voice became soft, yet it was filled with sorrow and regret.

"Perhaps, Henry…in another time and another place, we could have had a life together. But the heart has a mind of its own. Despite all of his faults, and there were many, I loved Jack, and I mourn his passing. You are an honorable gentleman that deserves better than the woman who stands before you, because in the end, I am as flawed as the man I married. I wish you well."

With that, Beryl turned her back and faced the window once more, her eyes swelling with tears. Henry let out a long sigh of resignation. He was nearly out of the room when he stopped and said his last goodbye to the woman he had loved.

"Mr. Holmes has made the authorities aware of your refusal to take part in my…demise. I shall see to it that my written statement absolving you of blame is read into the minutes at your trial in London. As to the previous matter of Sir Charles' death, I believe you would do well to throw yourself at the mercy of the court. Goodbye Beryl."

He closed the door behind him as he left and made his way to the front office. The constable had somehow found the correspondence he had been searching for and was dutifully filling out a report. He put his pen down to speak.

"I see that you are finished with your visit, Sir Henry."

"Yes, thank you so much for your kindness, sergeant. I won't forget it. If there is anything that I can do for YOU, please do not hesitate to call upon me."

"Well… now that you mention, it, there is the little matter of Selden, sir."

"Selden…the convict?"

"Yes, sir; the authorities at Princetown don't want any part of him, sir, his body, that is, now that he's dead and all. Would you be willing to sign a form releasing him to you for burial?"

"I would be happy to do so on behalf of Mr. and Mrs. Barrymore, and I will assist them in this matter. Where do I sign?"

"Right at the bottom of this here page by the X, if you don't mind. The body is in the basement of the undertaker, Mr. Williams, at the end of this street, waiting for some sort of resolution, as it were. Might I take a moment to say…I wish the VERY best of luck to you in the future, Sir Henry."

The squire was taken back briefly by the man's sincerity and paused for an instant before answering.

"Thank you so much, sergeant. I have the strangest feeling that I will need all the luck I can get."

CHAPTER 2

Visitors to Merripit House

"This is quite a pretty grim landscape if you ask me, Inspector Lestrade. I can't imagine why anyone would care to live out here in such a bleak, depressing setting."

The uniformed officer then shook his head in disbelief and turned his raincoat's collar up around his neck as a quick rush of air smacked both men squarely in the face. The two figures staggered for a moment and pushed on ahead, following the carriage rutted dirt lane towards the top of a hill, where a fork in the road was waiting.

"One man's meat is another man's poison, I always say Bleeker. There are a number of farms and houses scattered about Dartmoor. Some people just enjoy the solitude, I imagines. One thing is certain; you're more apt to avoid a row with your neighbor if he's several miles away. Now go on ahead a bit and tell me if you can catch a glimpse of Merripit House. I don't want to take the wrong road and lose valuable time."

The officer raised an eyebrow but said nothing for the moment. He forged on to the top of the hill, peered around, and turned back to face his superior.

"I see it just to the left, Inspector. It's only about half a mile off."

It was then he muttered under his breath: "If you had remembered to bring the map, we would not have gotten off track in the first place."

Lestrade heard nothing of the added comment but saw his assistant's lips move, nonetheless. He made a mental note of it and decided to save his displeasure for another more appropriate time. He adjusted the bowler hat on his head so that it would not blow away and caught up with his charge at the top of the hill.

"Well, it's not Baskerville Hall, but from what I see of it so far, Merripit House appears to be a converted farmhouse. I notice some renovations, and an addition here and there. I would venture to guess that it's one of the nicer homes on Dartmoor."

"That wouldn't take very much effort, Inspector. From the little I've seen it's a hard life on the moor."

"You'll get no argument from me on that account, Bleeker. Have you got the house keys that Miss Stapleton or rather, the widow Baskerville gave to you at her questioning?"

"Right here in my coat pocket, Inspector. That's all well and good, but WHAT exactly are we looking for? We already know that her husband frightened Sir Charles to death by way of the hound he bought, and tried unsuccessfully to do the same to Sir Henry until Mr. Holmes shot the beast. Isn't the case closed?"

"First off, remember that I was with Mr. Holmes when WE foiled that plan, Bleeker. Second, this is not a continuing investigation against Rodger Baskerville, but rather, we are here to search the place to see if there is any further evidence for or against his wife."

The two men walked up to the front of the house. Before them stood a wide, wooden door that had recently been painted a brilliant white. An inlaid stained glass viewing window beckoned them to look inside, but the interior was dark and foreboding.

"Well, she did offer us her ring of keys. Do you think she will get off, Inspector?"

"That's hard to say."

He paused and slapped one hand into other as he rattled off his observations.

"Let us consider the facts as we know them; she could plead ignorance to the first murder plot, and her abuse at the hands of her husband during the second will obviously work in her favor. But there is the glaring fact that Rodger was a Baskerville and changed his name when they pulled up stakes to move closer to the Baskerville estate…and its unsuspecting heirs.

When you top that all off with the ruse she went along with when she pretended to be the sister of her own husband, then one could say that she's in a bit of a pickle. Knowing the English system of justice as I do Bleeker, I doubt that she will walk away a free woman to go on about her business. I envision some jail time in her future, but ironically enough, how much may very well depend on the written testimony of Sir Henry himself, poor chap. I understand from Doctor Watson that he was completely smitten with her, and she made no real attempt to stop that from developing."

"I think I've found the right key for this here lock, Inspector. Let me give it a slow turn. There we go, I've got it."

The door opened smoothly and quietly, as though unwilling to disturb the silence that pervaded the rooms of the vacant, two story structure. The Scotland Yarders unconsciously paused for a moment.

"All right now, Bleeker, in we go. There's an entire house to poke around in, and I want to get back to Grimpen before dark."

"Still worried about the REAL hound of hell, Inspector?"

Lestrade pursed his lips and gave off a sharp look of disgust, much like a teacher who had caught a student cheating on an exam.

"Enough of that now, enough of that; Mr. Holmes and I have put THAT legend to rest once and for all."

Bleeker gave him a queer look before responding. "I'm not so sure, Inspector. The Baskerville's hound story has been around for quite some time, according to the villagers hereabouts. Most legends have a basis in fact somewhere in the distant past. Perhaps…"

Lestrade shut down the conversation. "There's no perhaps about it! Stop this nonsense and go on about your business. You take the two second floor bedrooms, and be quick about it. I'll poke around on ground level. My lord, it's awfully cold in this house, now that no one's living in it. Even that old servant has run off. It wouldn't surprise me if he too played a hand in the doings of last week."

The two men peeled off as they entered the foyer. Bleeker made for the wide mouth staircase that lay straight ahead, while Lestrade turned to his right into the dining room. While the exterior of the house was a bit more than modest in appearance, the interior portrayed the perfect touch of Victorian elegance and wealth. Fine furnishings were everywhere in sight, along with tasteful wallpaper, brush stroked paintings, and luxurious rugs.

Lestrade first poked around in the drawers of an expansive hutch, found nothing of interest, and made his way into the living room, where he rummaged through end table drawers and searched behind books that had been neatly lined up within a built in book case situated along a far wall. He could hear Bleeker's footsteps above him as his assistant tread softly from room to room, with slight creaks emanating from the ceiling as he walked, giving away his location.

Within a short time, both men were back together. There was no need for Lestrade to question his man about any successful finds. He would have heard a shout if anything of value had been discovered. As for himself, he had fared no better in the quest for further evidence, and as he glanced out a laced curtain window to a dusky moor, he had the uneasy feeling that all their efforts would be wasted.

"Well, me lad, all that's left is Rodger's study here, which may have the potential of being the most promising location of all, if you ask me. As I recall from my conversation with Miss Stapleton, I mean Mrs. Baskerville, it should be here behind these closed pocket doors. Let me give them a pull and see what we can come up with; cross your fingers."

Lestrade grasped the gold plated knobs and pulled the doors apart with an effortless tug. They in turn rolled away from each other and quickly disappeared inside the walls on opposite sides. What lay before them were indeed strange sights to behold, even by the current bohemian standards of what was Victorian England.

"Well strike me up a gum tree, Bleeker. Will you have a look at all THIS?"

"I must say I've never seen the likes of it in all my life, Inspector…at least, not in somebody's home, that is. It's like walking into a bloomin' museum!"

"It IS a museum, of sorts. This Stapleton was what they calls a naturalist. It would stand to reason that he would collect items from the surrounding moor and study them in depth. Look here…a skull, probably from one of those stone huts that Dr. Mortimer claims were the houses of neo..neolith…neolithic man, that's it.

And take a peek at this model of that spot on the moor near here; small rock fragments placed in a circle, probably chipped off the larger stone behemoths we passed on the way here. Notice how they appear to be placed in alignment, much like their larger counterparts in the wild long ago?"

"Nothing gets past you, Inspector. Blimey, this collection here looks like it took quite some time to acquire."

Lestrade spied Bleeker pick up an object in front of him. "What have you got there?"

"It's a case full of beautiful dead butterflies, spread wings out in row after row. There are names under each one. Let me see what I can make out." Bleeker smiled, as he knew Lestrade would be annoyed.

"These are all from the Frit-ill-ary Species: there's the High Brow, the Pearl Bordered, the Marsh, the Dark Green, and the Silver Washed. I have to admit they look alike to me sir—a lot of orange coloring, with black dots on the wings, and…"

"Enough of that, now; I don't give a scotch farthing about any bloomin' butterflies! Check that roll top desk over there in the corner. It appears to be his work space. If we are to find any further clues, I'll wager they'll be waiting for us inside."

Bleeker raised the roll top and began searching through the cubby holes. Lestrade came up from behind him and began rummaging through the deep sets of drawers. His face brightened when he came to the last drawer and plucked out a soft, dark object.

"Half a mo; here's the fake beard that Stapleton must have used when he was in London shadowing Sir Henry. Take THAT, Mr. Sherlock Holmes!"

"Ah…that's fine and dandy, Inspector, but I don't see how that ties in with his sister's, er, wife's complicity in the attempted murder of Sir Henry."

Lestrade's moment of joy was short lived. He suddenly realized his false triumph and meekly put the beard in his back pocket with a sigh.

"It doesn't tie her in at all, Bleeker. It only reinforces Mr. Holmes' theory. I suppose our investigation here is at an end.

Let's be getting on back to Grimpen. I could use a meal and a good night's rest before returning to London with our prisoner."

The men shuffled dejectedly out of the house with Bleeker locking the door behind him. The two returned to the road and began their long walk back to the village as twilight settled in upon the moor. Lestrade broke the silence.

"Mrs. Baskerville didn't appear to be particularly upset when told of the death of her husband the night he tried to kill Sir Henry. In fact, she didn't register much emotion at all when she was informed that he most certainly met his demise in the great Grimpen Mire. She may be a striking figure of a woman, but she's one hard case, that one. Don't be deceived by appearances."

"That's an awful way to die, Inspector. I don't care how bad a bloke you are; sinking slowly into that mucky bog, surrounded by nothing but the darkness and your own screams; it makes me shudder just to think of it."

"He got what he deserved that one. It was justice from Providence, I calls it. Now let's get a move on. I'm feeling the cold in my bones already and we haven't even lost sight of the house yet."

Inspector Lestrade missed more than incriminating clues on this excursion. Not more than a hundred feet from the house, nestled discreetly behind a low stone wall, sat a pale, shivering man who everyone thought to be dead. A quick peek over the moss covered granite revealed what he had been waiting for. The two Scotland Yarders had passed out of sight and sound. Now was the time. With a great effort, Jack Stapleton bounded over the wall and made his way tentatively to what only about a week ago had been his former home.

Even though night was fast approaching and the moor was gray and desolate, he kept the house between him and the road, letting it act as a buffer as he reached the back door and fumbled with the keys in order to gain entry. With a hard shove, the door swung open and he stepped back into his former world of ease and comfort.

Although the kitchen was dark, Stapleton had no problem rushing straight to the food pantry. With trembling fingers he unscrewed the nearest jar on the shelf and put it to his lips. It contained peaches in heavy syrup. He slurped it hungrily, devouring the fruit sections and liquid en masse until the jar was completely drained. With closed eyes and a deep sigh, he leaned with his back against the shelving for a few moments to collect his thoughts.

The last week had been quite an ordeal; one that he could never have imagined would come to pass. With the plan to murder Sir Henry and steal his inheritance foiled at the last moment by the meddling of Sherlock Holmes, Stapleton was forced to take his chances in the Grimpen Mire. Although he had cleverly staked a pathway through the morass, he had never attempted it at night; and yet, he still found a way through the darkness to the abandoned tin mine where he had kept the huge dog that was meant to be the instrument of Sir Henry's death.

While his disappearance convinced the authorities that he had met his end in a deep and silent bog, the situation forced him to live on the very scraps and brackish water that he had left for the hound he had purchased. It was a bitter irony for him to ponder as the wind whipped through the mine and nearly froze him to the bone, but it was also a strong motivation to still pre-vail.

He would not be denied despite the setback, which he surmised might also have included a betrayal by his own wife. Leaving her bound and bruised in the upstairs bedroom was not a situation that she could easily have explained away even if she had wanted to remain loyal. Her absence from their house also suggested to him that she may have cooperated with the police in some fashion in an effort to avoid an excessive sentence.

No, Beryl was gone from him forever. But now was not the time to think of her. His chief concerns at this time were staying alive and remaining "dead" to the world. Stapleton climbed the stairs to the second floor linen closet and carefully removed three large pillow cases. In the first one he placed several woolen bed spreads. Then it was into the master bedroom, where he stuffed as much winter clothing as possible into the second.

Although it was still the fall season, the harsh night environment of the moor and the mine had proved nearly unbearable. He found several heavy weight winter coats, and wisely decided to save room in the last pillow case by simply putting them both on over his now mud stained suit. Finally, it was back to the kitchen pantry, where he loaded up on canned meats and mason jars sealed tight with vegetables and preserves.

Fire place striking matches were reverently slipped into one of his coat pockets to complete his first haul of the evening. He was well aware that his trip later on would be more difficult. Jugs of water would be the prized items, and he surmised that their sheer weight and volume would tax his strength to the limit.

Rodger Baskerville of Costa Rica, alias Mr. Vandeleur of Yorkshire, alias Jack Stapleton of Dartmoor, did not consider for a moment that he was a beaten man, not by a long shot. All he needed was time to sort things out. With everyone, even the great Sherlock Holmes under the impression that he was a dead man, he was sure to have that precious commodity.

Stapleton began the slow, arduous trek back across the moor to the tin mine within the Grimpen Mire with a steely look of determination. However, not even in his wildest dreams could he have convinced himself that something hidden within the pitch black moor was watching him with great interest.

CHAPTER 3

Joy In Grimpen Village

R everend Musgrave squinted into the faded mirror in the corner of his sparsely furnished room and began to sing a very poor version of "A Mighty Fortress Is Our God." He gently jockeyed a white clerical collar around his neck until it felt fairly comfortable, then turned to his cat to continue the serenade. He was a thin, white haired old gentleman who had become frail in recent years.

Unfortunately, singing was not one of the vicar's strong-points. With its head cocked and ears now drawn back, the tabby gave a quick look to the door and flew off the wicker chair's seat cushion, making a hasty retreat to the blessed silence of the rectory's first floor sitting parlor.

The reverend sighed in resignation as he made his way care-fully down the stairs to the coat stand in the hallway to put on his gray woolen jacket. Although he was well aware of his vocal deficiencies, he could not help but be happy. Tonight was Grimpen's Fall Festival, and he had some very important news to relay to the village's inhabitants, news that would touch each and every one of them for the better. As he opened the door of the rectory to leave, a woman's pleasant voice rang out from the kitchen.

"Reverend, don't forget your hat, if you please, sir. There may be a bit of a chill in the air later, and I don't want you to catch your death."

Musgrave was momentarily startled, then quickly scooped the hat from the stand and placed it on his head before answering with a smile.

"I already have it on, Mrs. Beale. No need to worry. Will you be coming to the festivities later on?"

"Oh, yes, sir. I'm just keeping an eye on a shepherd's pie that looks to be about ready to come out of the oven. Once I have that under control, I will go back home and return to town with the family."

"Glad to hear it. See you later then; I'm off."

He smiled and muttered quietly to himself; "Wonderful housekeeper, Mrs. Beale. I daresay don't know what I would do without her. And her shepherd's pie is a feast fit for a bishop."

Musgrave made the short walk to the village center. It was so short that he could watch the festivities from the front steps of the rectory if he so chose. But this was going to be a festival like no other Grimpen had had before, and he was bursting with pride to be part of it. He had not gone ten paces before he was acknowledged.

"Well, hello, reverend. I'm glad to see you could make it."

It was Cassidy, the beer scented village lamplighter, amongst other minor municipal duties, beginning his rounds as the sun began to set behind the tors. Musgrave responded with a bible verse.

"And God said, let there be light. You are doing the Lord's work, Mr. Cassidy, even if you don't realize it. By the way, I hope to SEE YOU tomorrow at Sunday service. Can I count on your presence?"

Cassidy did not miss a beat. Old Musgrave had been trying to reel him in for years without success, but this was one big fish that knew how to spit the hook. He looked thoughtfully at the vicar before responding with a glance to the heavens.

"Well, reverend…as my sainted mother used to say to me: Raymond, my son, there's a thin line between Saturday night and Sunday morning. So, I'll give it my best shot, sir, although I can't guarantee anything, you understand."

Trying desperately to hide his amusement, Musgrave turned away and continued into the village square which was starting to bustle with excitement. All of the businesses were decorated with Union Jack colored bunting and moor flowers. Numerous tables and booths were being placed around the village square and filled with all manner of delicacies, a four piece band was tuning up in front of an inviting village pub named The Rat and Raven, and in the center of it all, a wooden speakers platform and accompanying chairs was being eyeballed and properly levelled by the local carpenter and his son.

Villagers came pouring in from every direction as if on cue. It would take a bit more time for some of the outlying farmers and their families to arrive, but this was shaping up to be one of the most well attended Fall Festivals in many a year. Even the brooding Dartmoor weather appeared to get in the spirit of things, as the approaching night air was calm and unusually mild. This would certainly help to prolong the festivities, much to the delight of those selling food, spirits, and trinkets.

While adults greeted one another, mingling about the booths and tables as music filled the air, children ran off in small groups to play at the gaming tables to test their skills. Reverend Musgrave caught the eye of the corpulent village mayor, Mr. Sexton, and the two were soon off in a corner and engaged in deep conversation. Whenever someone would come by for a quick chat, they would stop talking and greet the person cheerfully, but as soon as the coast was clear, they would return to their conversation with renewed vigor.

The celebration grew louder as the night went on, while strangely enough Musgrave and Sexton began to appear apprehensive and nervous. The mayor pulled out his pocket watch on several occasions and shook his head with dismay, while the vicar kept glancing at the main road out of town. Finally, both men breathed a sigh of relief as a black coach with the Baskerville crest emblazoned on its side door appeared over a hill and made its way into the square.

The driver turned off quietly into a side street and pulled up on the reigns of the panting old horse, much to its delight. He climbed down, quickly adjusting his waistcoat and hat before assuming an erect posture prior to opening the coach door. Out bounded Sir Henry Baskerville....covered in mud. In fact, a closer inspection showed that both men were thoroughly splattered with the thick brown paste from head to foot.

A look of bemusement wafted over the young squire's face as the locals stopped what they were doing and stared at him in disbelief. He waved shyly to the crowd then quickly made his way to the two bewildered community leaders, whom he met with a smile, and an explanation.

"SO sorry I'm late, gentlemen. I make it a point to be punctual, but this could not be helped. A most extraordinary thing happened on the way from Baskerville Hall. As we were going round a steep bend in the road, one of the rear wheels suddenly began to wobble terribly. Before Perkins had a chance to stop the carriage, the wheel popped off its axle, turning the carriage nearly over on its side.

Most fortunately, it wound up resting cockeyed against a large tree otherwise we both could have been seriously hurt...even killed for that matter. Perkins did nearly fall off, but he was able to hold onto the iron bar by the edge of the seat. The poor man is beside himself with remorse, but he insists that he performed a thorough check of the carriage early this morning, and cannot understand how this could possibly have happened. Of course, it has been in my family for many years, so a defect due to age is a distinct possibility.

For my part, I slammed against the inside of the door, but it did not pop open. As I said, that old tree stopped our fall. Perhaps I shall officially name it Sir Henry's Tree, in honor if it saving my life. If I had been thrown from the carriage and it then landed on me... well, I would not be here talking with you now. It took us the devil's own time to get that wheel back on its axle. That's why we are in such a muddy state of affairs; there's the truth of it."

Reverend Musgrave bowed his head, made the sign of the cross, and mumbled what surely was a prayer before looking back up at the squire.

"Thank God for his blessings upon you, Sir Henry. He still has important tasks for you to perform, and we will make certain that some of them are revealed tonight. Come... let us step up to the platform to address the villagers."

The three men made their way through the crowd to the middle of the square. Mayor Sexton knew he had a difficult task on his hands trying to gather the attention of the throng, as many were literally dancing in the streets, no doubt as a result of the various types of spirits being sold in the tavern. While Sir Henry and the reverend sat patiently on the chairs behind him, Sexton raised his hands and shouted out greetings in an effort to attract attention, but that failed miserably.

The squire leaned over to Reverend Musgrave with a suggestion, and the vicar quickly hailed the mayor to come back and sit down, which he did. With that, Musgrave rose from his chair, stepped forward, and stood with his arms outstretched. Within a minute, the crowd was silent and gathered around the platform, even lamplighter Cassidy, who was in the process of draining a pint of bitters. The vicar cleared his throat as though he were about to deliver one of his Sunday sermons, then let fly with his nasally voice.

"Dear friends, I hope you are all enjoying yourselves on this wonderful evening of fun and fellowship. I must first relay a secret; that I did offer up a weather prayer the day before yesterday for these festivities, and it would appear that the good Lord sought to answer it.

However, there is more to discover tonight than the good nature that is in all of us. You see, this is indeed going to be a special occasion, for we have with us as our honored guest for the very first time, Sir Henry Baskerville."

There was a moment of applause and modest "hear hears" all around. The handsome young squire stood up, smiled politely and waved his hand in the air before returning to his seat next to the beaming Mayor Sexton, who seemed to stare at Baskerville as though he were a well-cooked leg of mutton. Musgrave continued on.

"Now, it goes without saying to all here that our beloved Grimpen is a poor parish, and life on the moor does not lend itself to a wealth of riches. It has been well documented that our old steeple has been thoroughly infested with woodworms, and that only by the grace of God has a strong wind not blown it off the very roof of St. George's Church. Up to this point, even modest repairs have been out of the question due to the prohibitive costs involved, but that situation, I am happy to say, has now changed."

A buzz went out among the crowd, and people turned their heads about as though looking to one another for clarification before the vicar had a chance to finish.

"I am most gratified to say that St. George will be graced with an entirely NEW steeple, the cost of which shall be underwritten by our most generous benefactor, the church's new guardian angel as it were, Sir Henry Baskerville."

Hands clapped in appreciation, and grateful smiles were seen on the faces of the elder citizens who remembered the day that the present steeple was first erected. But Musgrave was not quite finished.

"Yes, that means a new tower, belfry, lantern, spire...and a gold cross at the very top for all to admire. And that's not all. Since we are getting a new steeple, the good squire has decided to use this opportunity to make any and all necessary repairs to the weather beaten roof as well. God bless you, Sir Henry!"

Church members hugged each other in sheer joy from the news, and some could be heard saying prayers of thanks. But the secular portion of the crowd, which up to this point had only offered tepid but polite appreciation, was not to be ignored on this night. Once Reverend Musgrave took his seat, Mayor Sexton rose to speak next with all of his oratorical skill.

"Good citizens of Grimpen and the outlying moor, Reverend Musgrave, Sir Henry; it is with great pleasure that I stand before this evening."

There was a short pause. Cassidy used the opportunity to let out a long, hard belch, which pleased the many children in the crowd to no end. Meanwhile, the adults shook their heads with disgust. They did not have to look around to discover who committed the offense. Sexton pretended to ignore the insult, politician that he was, and continued on with his speech.

"The good news is not over my friends. You have all heard Reverend Musgrave's wonderful revelations concerning the future of St. George's Church. Now, Sir Henry has extended that bright future to the village of Grimpen itself!"

Sexton glanced around for a rousing cheer from the assemblage, but as he had not bothered to go into any detail, the faces looking up at him were blank and silent. He instantly recognized his faux pas and began to blurt out information.

"The roads in and out of the village and outer farms are the very life's blood of Dartmoor. Over the years, some have, in sections, become nothing more than muddy quagmires not much better than the Grimpen Mire itself. This has put a severe strain on commerce in and out of the area, and has also led to a decrease in profits.

Well, Sir Henry has contracted with an outside firm, from London mind you, to come to us and rebuild what has washed away over the years. Turtleback center grading will be re-established, stone underlayment will be shored up, and most importantly, the outer side ditches, which have filled in with silt over time, will be dug out and expanded to drain the rainwater properly once again."

The faces on the merchants began to brighten, but there was more.

"In addition, all, and I repeat all, of our nearby bridges, be they stone clapper, wooden clam, or large post, will be inspected by Sir Henry's representatives for repair or replacement as they deem necessary! I say that calls for a rousing three cheers for Sir Henry! Are you with me?"

The crowd whooped in unison as if on cue, with hats flying in the air: "Hip hip..hooray! Hip hip.. hooraay! Hip hip..hooraaaay!"

Sexton smiled and waved his arms in the air. One would almost think that he was the reason for so much joy; but as a politician, he was used to taking credit where none was due. He turned around and beckoned Sir Henry to step forward to say a few words.

Reverend Musgrave, sitting patiently all that time at the rear of the platform, deftly lunged forward, grabbed the mayor's coattails, and proceeded to reel him in. The vicar could not help but think that this particular catch was equal to the finest trout he had ever stuffed in his creel.

CHAPTER 4

A Chance Encounter

Sir Henry smiled and bowed repeatedly to the excited crowd showering him with cheers and affection. He appeared genuinely embarrassed by the sudden attention, and the more he blushed and fidgeted about on the platform, the more the people's new found love for him grew.

This was no pompous land baron who thought himself better than the common Dartmoor folk. He was one with them, and they with him. To the poor village of Grimpen, he was literally a gift from heaven. Finally, with some entreaties from the mayor, the noise began to slacken, and the squire cleared his throat to speak.

"Friends...good citizens of Grimpen and beyond, I thank you with all my heart for the manner in which you have accepted me into your community. Just a few weeks ago I was a total stranger, brought here by way of a terrible tragedy that resulted in the untimely death of my poor Uncle Charles.

I understand that he too was deeply committed to this region and to the people in it, with many good works performed by him from behind the scenes as it were. Yet you all knew who was responsible. He wanted no credit, no fanfare. In short, he was a truly honorable man. In hindsight, I wish that I could have had the opportunity to know him better.

Now that Mr. Sherlock Holmes has finally cleared up the mystery surrounding the hound of the Baskervilles, I can think of no better way of honoring Sir Charles' memory than by continuing his philanthropic endeavors for the good of all. I hope in the coming months to get to know all of you better… upon my return."

The last few words left people scratching their heads and looking about. The new squire had barely just arrived to his ancestral home. Even the vicar and mayor looked stunned by the news. Sir Henry continued on.

" I realize that this may come as a bit of a shock, what with my having just recently arrived to Dartmoor, but to be frank with you all, the recent episode that culminated in my near death has left my nerves in a bad state, I am afraid. My good friend and neighbor Dr. Mortimer has suggested that a short trip would be just the tonic I need to pick up my spirits, and I must confess that I agree with him wholeheartedly.

He has relatives in Edinburgh that he has desired to visit for quite some time. James has graciously invited me to accompany him on a land journey through Scotland and its Highlands, then finish up sailing to the Orkney Islands and finally, to the Isle of Skye. We are leaving in a few days, but plan to return in early December.

Well…enough of my prattling on; let us get back to the festival, and when I do return, please stop by the hall when you are on the moor. It is open to friends of my uncle, and to all of you, my new neighbors. God bless you."

The squire could not have made a better impression. His heartfelt speech and unassuming air won the crowd over completely. Unfortunately, this new found popularity made it impossible for him to go more than a few paces without having his hand vigorously shaken and squeezed like a lemon. Soon his fingers began to ache and throb, but he hid his pain and did not refuse a single greeting despite the discomfort.

As the night drew to a close, Henry noticed a lone, plainly dressed woman off to one side, standing on the outside of a cluster of revelers. She did not interact with them to any great extent, nor did they go out of their way to speak with her either.

Although she was attractive in a modest sort of way, her drawn face and lusterless eyes gave off the appearance of some recent deep sorrow. Perhaps that was why the villagers kept a respectable distance from her. His curiosity eventually got the better of him; with Reverend Musgrave far off and unable to act as a go between, he approached her with caution as a prelude in his effort to strike up an introductory conversation.

"You certainly have picked a quiet spot to observe the proceedings, but I daresay you will enjoy yourself much better if you move to the center of the village square."

Despite his sincere attempt at diplomacy, the woman was completely taken aback. Her lips parted and her eyes stared at him in disbelief. After several seconds, she lowered her head ever so slightly and began to speak with great effort.

"I am happy to see that you decided to attend the festival, Sir Henry."

"It would appear that you have the better of me, my good woman. You know my name, but I do not know yours."

The woman looked visibly stung by the seemingly innocent statement. She took a deep breath and responded in a tone that almost made him think that she felt ashamed to be in his presence.

"Oh, that's not entirely true, Sir Henry, although I daresay the Baskervilles are none the better for it. You see…I am Laura Lyons"

Now it was Sir Henry's turn to be startled.

"You…do you mean to say that YOU are the mysterious LL that Mr. Holmes and Dr. Watson spoke of?"

"Yes, Sir Henry, the same LL that wrote to your Uncle Charles to meet me that horrible night just a short time ago in the yew alley at Baskerville Hall. As you well know, Jack...I mean Mr. Stapleton, used me to lure Sir Charles to his death. Unfortunately, his plan worked to perfection."

She sighed, dropped her shoulders, and stared off into the distance before continuing. It was obvious that the conversation was painful to her.

"While the authorities, that is, Mr. Holmes and Inspector Lestrade, have seen fit to clear me of any misconduct, nevertheless I feel partly responsible by being taken in by such a horrible man. In the most literal sense, I was bait for his trap. I certainly thought that after the many trials and tribulations I had endured with my estranged husband and the subsequent shunning by my father that I could never feel any lower...but now I do."

Sir Henry was deeply touched by the poor woman's plight. He responded not with an expression of pity, but one of sympathy.

"It would appear that both of us have been taken in by that rascal Stapleton, Mrs. Lyons. What you may not know is that I proceeded to fall in love with Beryl, his sister, or I should say his wife. Although she would take no part in the plot against me, she continued the deception.

I believe that was most bitter pill to swallow, to know that I had been so terribly misled in such a manner, and for such a vile purpose. So, I daresay that fate has made us kindred spirits in a strange way, wouldn't you agree, Mrs. Lyons?"

"Well, I suppose one could certainly say that to be entirely true, Sir Henry. Then you...you harbor me no ill will?"

"Not in the least! Mr. Holmes happened to mention that he called upon you at your residence in Coombe Tracey to clear up some of the mystery surrounding my family. How did you arrive at the festival, Mrs. Lyons?"

"Why, I walked, Sir Henry; it's but a few miles, a mere stretch of the legs, as the people are wont to say hereabouts."

"Well, I for one am tired and ready to leave. My nerves are not quite what they should be, after this hound business. May I offer you a ride back in my carriage, Mrs. Lyons? The Dartmoor roads are pitch black at night for those travelling on foot, and to be honest, I could do with a bit of company right now."

"This IS most kind of you, Sir Henry. I would be flattered to accompany you, if you would but call me Laura."

"And so I shall, Laura….but only if you would agree to call me Henry."

She smiled approvingly and the two of them made their way towards the carriage Perkins had parked around one of the side streets. With any luck, he would not have strayed far away, but that was asking a great deal, as there was food and drink aplenty.

Among the happy revelers, eyebrows raised and tongues began to wag at the sight of this odd couple fate had brought together under such terrible circumstances. Reverend Musgrave caught sight of them quietly leaving the festival and looked on with a strange fascination.

However, to his complete surprise, he discovered that he was not displeased with this startling new development. There was something about this couple walking and talking side by side that seemed quite natural, and it appeared that the villagers were of the same sentiment. The Lord does work in mysterious ways, he thought to himself as he shook his head with a wry smile…VERY mysterious.

"Your uncle offered financial help to free me from my present situation, Henry. English law does not generally favor the side of women, especially those embroiled in scandalous divorce cases. But I am adamant to rid myself of the wretched shadow that my absent husband has cast over my life."

She stopped and glanced at him with a careworn face. "It's ironic, is it not? Sir Charles offered me hope, while Jack Stapleton offered me marriage. Now, both men are dead, and I am left alone once again with a man who refuses to grant my release."

"Do not give up hope at this late juncture, Laura. When I return from my trip with Dr. Mortimer, I shall contact my solicitors in London to look into the matter more thoroughly. I believe that my late uncle would approve of such a move."

"You would do that...for me, a stranger?"

"After my return...perhaps we shall no longer remain strangers."

As the two made their way slowly past the village church, a large black shape watched them silently with great interest from behind a broken headstone in the adjoining cemetery. It lifted its head in the air and sniffed long and deep, as though recognizing by scent an old acquaintance.

CHAPTER 5

221B

The great detective stood in front of the fireplace, gazing at the crackling red embers of a dying fire. He glanced up and reached for the woven Persian slipper filled with tobacco that was perched on top of the mantle, and then proceeded to stuff his calabash with a fragrant mixture, at least by his own standards. His companion sat at a desk nearby and began to whine.

"Dash it all Holmes, must you smoke that filthy stuff? It smells like an old sock."

Holmes turned with a smile and responded with a tone of fake pomposity as he proceeded to light the pipe.

"My dear Watson, do you not remember that I once wrote a monograph covering over one hundred and forty distinct types of tobacco ash?"

"Are you MAD? How could I possibly FORGET it? The room was filled with smoke at all hours of the day and night; cigars, pouches and cigarettes scattered all about, and you gazing under that microscope all the while. At one point dear Mrs. Hudson thought her house was on fire; nearly frightened her half to death, poor woman. I like a pipe now and again myself,

Holmes, but I must admit you forced me to take refuge at my club on more than one occasion."

"Ah, but don't forget Watson, without the publication of my monograph, you would never have discovered that delightful Arcadia mixture that you now smoke so frequently."

Watson mumbled something under his breath and went back to writing on a sheet of paper. A short stack of completed sheets sat at a corner of the desk. Holmes spied them and surmised their meaning. He closed his eyes and let out a sigh of resignation before speaking again to his colleague.

"If you feel that you must continue in your quest to act as my Boswell, Watson, I do hope that you would concentrate your energies on the analytical reasoning involved in my cases, and not on the sensational or romantic elements that are so popular to the readers of The Strand Magazine. You do have a way of going off on tangents, I am afraid. Facts, Watson, always stick to the facts, and they will see you through."

Watson looked up with an uncommon look of satisfaction, so much so that it took Holmes by complete surprise.

"If you must know, I am in the process of doing just that, Holmes. The problem is that there are so many OF them."

"Which case have you decided to chronicle for the ages now, if I may be so bold as to ask?"

"Why, the one we've barely just finished, of course! I have decided to call it…The Hound of the Baskervilles. What do you think of the title?"

He looked at Holmes anxiously for the slightest sign of approval, but he was to be disappointed yet again.

"Not one of your better ones, I am afraid, although I am sure it will titillate your readers. I must say that it was a most interesting case from my perspective as a detective, particularly the supernatural elements that permeated the whole nasty business. Of course, as soon as Sir Henry's boot was stolen at the hotel, I was ready to discard that possible aspect altogether."

Watson sat back in his chair for a moment.

"That quickly, eh? You don't believe in the possibility of the supernatural do you Holmes?"

His friend paused for a moment before answering, and his reply sounded almost melancholy.

"I neither believe nor disbelieve, Watson, but I have yet to come upon a case where I could conclusively prove that the supernatural WAS involved."

He then pointed his pipe at the doctor.

"Until that time arrives, I must remain the ardent skeptic, as it were. My scientific mind simply has no choice in the matter."

"Well Holmes, as Shakespeare once said: There are more things in heaven and earth, Horatio, than are dreamt of in your philosophy."

"Actually, a purist would remark Hamlet said that, Watson. By the by, I believe Mrs. Hudson is arriving with our breakfast."

With a few quick steps, Holmes reached the door and opened it as a short, heavy set woman reached the top of the stairs holding a tray draped over with white linen that curiously appeared to match her hair color. She smiled broadly and whisked her way directly to a table that was cluttered with stacks of books and newspapers.

"Really, Mr. Holmes, this table is a sight. How can I serve a proper breakfast? Should I take it that you wish to eat standing up?"

Holmes laughed as he adjusted his smoking jacket.

"Now, now, Mrs. Hudson; I shall make space available for your repast. Just give me a moment."

He proceeded to erect a tower of the books in one corner of the table, then scooped up the newspapers and placed them on the seat of a high backed wicker chair. Watson had already seen fit to seat himself and was eyeing the tray with great anticipation. Holmes relieved Mrs. Hudson of her burden, placed it directly in the middle of the table, and with a final flourish, tugged sharply on the linen to reveal the first meal of the day.

A large bowl of hot porridge was the main dish, accompanied by soft boiled eggs, toast, fruit, and a steaming pot of tea. Watson smiled at the welcome sight and began to ladle out scoops of the porridge, topping it off with a splash of cream. Holmes, aware that Mrs. Hudson forever fretted over his lack of appetite, chose an egg and tapped off the top of the shell with feigned enthusiasm. Mrs. Hudson smiled. All was well in her world now.

As she left the room and headed down the stairs, she stopped on the way to have a brief but not so friendly conversation with a visitor. The two men listened intently. Watson became concerned for a moment, but Holmes waived him off with a smile. He already knew the identity of their caller. A few seconds later there was a knock at the door. Holmes glanced at Watson and raised his voice in response.

"Come in, Inspector Lestrade, do come in."

A tall, well-built gentleman sporting a thin mustache and wearing a tan raincoat entered the room with a scowl on his face. Nipping at his heels was the equally unhappy Mrs. Hudson, who was glaring at the back of his head with a vengeance.

"Mr. Holmes, Dr. Watson, I told him that you were having breakfast and were not to be disturbed, but he insisted on barging his way in like a mad bull. I AM sorry."

Holmes responded quickly with words of re-assurance to their motherly landlady.

"No need to apologize, Mrs. Hudson. I'm sure that Inspector Lestrade has a very sound and logical reason for barging in, don't you Inspector?"

Lestrade knew he was being played, but he was in need of Holmes' assistance, and therefore could not retaliate as he would have liked. He answered directly and to the point.

"Right you are, Mr. Holmes. I'm here on official Scotland Yard business."

He looked Mrs. Hudson and remarked "Just a little matter of MURDER."

She spun around and left the room in a huff, spouting something unintelligible as she went down the stairs. But now it was Watson who put on a scowl.

"Come now, Lestrade; we have just recently returned from Dartmoor. It's not just Sir Henry that needs to recoup. Keep in mind that Holmes was living out on that ghastly moor for days, and…"

Holmes interjected before his friend could go on.

"Which brings me to a few questions in that regard; you brought Mrs. Stapleton back with you to London, did you not?"

"That we did, Mr. Holmes. She is awaiting trial at this very moment."

"And did she happen to make any further incriminating statements?"

"No, Mr. Holmes, neither to me or Sergeant Bleeker, unfortunately. She is sticking to her original story. She did voluntarily give us the key to Merripit House, so that could count in her favor. We found nothing of value in the home that we could use at her trial. It's a very con..convo…"

Watson chimed in. "The word you are looking for is convoluted, Lestrade."

"Yes, that's it! Thank you Dr. Watson. As I was saying, it's
a very convoluted case, Mr. Holmes. There's really no way of
telling how this may end up for her. Now about the purpose of
my visit..."

Lestrade glanced down at the breakfast table and casually
picked up a piece of toast. Holmes shot him an annoying look
from his chair.

"Please have some, Inspector. You were saying something
about a murder?"

"Oh, yes. A body was found the other day on the front
steps of a house that had been burgled, although that is not
what's so strange. This residence, belonging to a Mr. Horace
Harker, is the third house to be robbed, but the one aspect that
ties them all in was that in each instance there was a smashed
plaster bust of Napoleon found on the floor. What do you
make of it, Mr. Homes?"

Watson gave out a chuckle. "Perhaps it's someone who
simply doesn't like Napoleon."

Holmes' eyes glistened at the comment. "I would be happy
to help you in this endeavor, Lestrade, but Dr. Watson is correct.
I need a few more days to rest up. In the meantime, continue
with your investigations, and keep in touch should there be any
further developments."

It was not exactly what Lestrade was hoping for, but he
accepted the summary judgment without complaint, and quietly left them to their now cold breakfast. Although Watson was
pleased that Holmes sided with him, he was surprised and suspicious that he had so summarily rebuffed the inspector.

"What's on your mind, Holmes? I've never seen you
reject an investigation so quickly. I would have thought that

the common thread...the broken busts of the little corporal, would have roused your interest in the case."

Holmes watched as Watson buttered a piece of toast and proceeded to slather jam over it. He raised an eyebrow before answering his old friend with a startling confession.

"The case does sound unusual to say the least, Watson, and I do quite intend to lend Lestrade my assistance; partly because he needs it poor chap, but also partly because I fear that there is a sinister reason for all that broken plaster."

"That's all well and good, Holmes, but why did you at least not have Lestrade send us with further information on the case up to this point? You were never one to just sit idly by. I would think that piecing together clues might be just the thing for you to occupy your time while you finish resting up."

Holmes put his hands together as though he was about to pray, then placed them in front of his lips and stared up at the ceiling for what seemed to the doctor to be an eternity. Finally, he broke free from his reverie to reveal his innermost thoughts, and his sober expression left no doubt that he was in deadly earnest.

"The knotty problem, Watson, is that I do not like to under-take a case until I am positively sure that I have solved the PRE-VIOUS one."

Watson was stunned; he dropped the toast jam side down into the porridge but paid no attention. He needed to make sure that there was no misunderstanding.

"Holmes, are you trying to tell me that this business at Baskerville Hall... the moor... Sir Henry...is NOT finished?"

"It MAY be finished."

Watson exploded; "MAY BE FINISHED? Dash it all, Holmes, stop beating about the bush and tell me what is going on!"

Holmes shook his head slowly from side to side, then rose to walk back to his calabash on the fireplace mantle. The pipe had since gone out; he re-lit it before measuring the words he was about to speak.

"I can say with a fair amount of certainty that the main participants of the plot have been exposed and dealt with. Let us consider them, Watson—the infamous hound of the Baskervilles has succumbed by my hand, and its master has fittingly died in the Grimpen Mire. Mrs. Stapleton, his wife, is now in a London prison, and the shadowy manservant Anthony, or probably Antonio if I am not mistaken, has disappeared and most likely left England altogether."

Watson became confused. "Yes, yes, I know all of that, Holmes. But who does that leave to harm Sir Henry? Surely you don't think that old Mr. Frankland, Dr. Mortimer, or even Barrymore was secretly involved in the plot with Stapleton?"

"Not at all, Watson, I don't believe any of them harbor the baronet any ill will; in fact, just the opposite. No…somehow, I feel that I might have, MIGHT, mind you, have overlooked a hidden player in this tragic play, and that person is still there, somewhere on Dartmoor. Two important questions remain for us…can this person still profit by the death of Sir Henry, and if so, does he still have the means to do it without drawing any suspicion upon himself?"

"If you still had doubts, then why did we leave in the first place?"

"Because I have no tangible proof of his existence, Watson. And the longer we stayed, the longer he would continue his ruse, most probably hiding in plain sight. We simply don't have a thread to tie him into the plot."

"I see what you mean, Holmes, but I feel somewhat guilty now about leaving Sir Henry without alerting him of your suspicions."

"That's all they are, Watson…suspicions. The man's health has been compromised by the recent affair. I didn't want to burden him any further, and besides, he is leaving with Dr. Mortimer shortly on their trip to Scotland. If there is another character involved, Sir Henry will be much safer away from Baskerville Hall than in it."

"So that's the end of it, Holmes? We leave the case dangling in the air? I can't believe that you would stand for such a resolution."

Holmes smiled and pointed to Watson's watch fob dangling out of his waistcoat. "I haven't. Kindly check your pocket watch and tell me the time, if you please."

"It's going on ten o'clock. Why do you ask?"

Holmes went over to the window, pulled back the drapes, and peered out across Baker Street.

"Unless I miss my guess, they should be arriving any minute now. Hello, they've just turned the corner. Good."

Watson was losing patience with his friend. Although well aware of the detective's penchant for keeping his own counsel, he found his temper beginning to get the best of him.

"They? Who on earth are you talking about Holmes, and what do THEY have to do with this case?"

"Do you remember the young lad Cartwright?"

"Of course; that's the boy who brought supplies and my letters to you while you were in hiding out on the moor without my knowledge."

"Right you are Watson. What you also do not know is that I gave him instructions to stay in Dartmoor for an additional week and to keep his eyes open while we returned to London. His week is now up. I sent word to Wiggins, one of my Baker

Street Irregulars, to fetch him directly when he returned to the messenger office where he is employed."

Watson's face puckered. "I don't see why you continue to bother with those wretched children...those irregulars as you call them, Holmes."

"Those wretches have been of great service to me in the past. They can go anywhere in London without drawing attention, which is more than I can say for the Scotland Yarders. Information is the cornerstone to victory, Watson."

Holmes had no sooner finished when the door opened and two boys entered; one was shabbily dressed, the other not much better. Watson greeted them sarcastically.

"Don't bother to knock, gentlemen. Come right in, won't you?"

Holmes waived him off and spoke directly to the older boy, who appeared to be about sixteen.

"I see that you have followed my instructions to the letter as always, Wiggins. Thank you for your assistance."

He drew a shilling from his pants pocket and placed it in the outstretched hand of the smiling youth, who then tipped his hat in gratitude.

"And do not forget to look into that other matter I spoke to you about the other day."

Wiggins responded eagerly as he made his exit. "Don't you worry about that, Mr. Holmes. I'll round up the rest of the irregulars and get on it straight away."

Holmes watched him with a fair amount of amusement as his young confederate left; then he drew his attention to Cartwright, who appeared to be several years younger. The lad seemed to be in awe of the fact that he was in the lodgings of the great Sherlock Holmes.

"So, Cartwright, I left you in Dartmoor with instructions to act as my eyes and ears. You may now give me your week's report."

The boy stood erect and recited his story with great earnest, as though the future of the British Empire depended on his very words.

"Well, I did exactly as you instructed, Mr. Holmes. I spent the first part of each day around the area of Baskerville Hall. I saw no strangers walking about the moor, at least no one who should not have been there. Mr. Frankland and Dr. Mortimer visited, along with two men who acted to me like they were policemen."

Holmes laughed. "That was undoubtedly Inspector Lestrade and his assistant, Sergeant Bleeker. What did I just tell you about the Scotland Yarders, Watson? You can pick them out of a crowd a mile off. Poor Lestrade; continue if you please, Cartwright."

"In the afternoons I stayed in the village. It seemed that the only bit of news people wanted to talk about was Sir Henry, if he was going to stay at the hall after what had happened. They were worried that he would go away and never come back.

In the early evenings I went out on the moor until it got so dark I could not see more than a few feet ahead, so help me, Mr. Holmes. I must admit, it is frightening out there alone, but I saw no one walking about. That's it, sir. I wish I could have come back with….oh, yes, there was one thing. On the last night I was there, after it got too dark on the moor, I went to the festival in Grimpen. Some men gave speeches, including Sir Henry. He looked very tired."

Watson broke in. "That does not seem to me to be of any significance. Sir Henry IS the local baronet. It stands to reason that he would be called upon to say a few appropriate words at various functions now and then."

"But that's not it, doctor. As he was walking about introducing himself to the people, he met a young woman who was by herself. I think that he offered her a ride in his carriage and off they went."

Holmes was intrigued. "A WOMAN, you say? Did you by chance happen to learn her name?

"No, sir, I did not. I did ask an old lady nearby, and she seemed to know, but would not give her name. All she would say was that the woman was not from Grimpen, thank heaven."

Ahhh, that narrows the beam, as it were. Thank you, Master Cartwright. You have done admirably. This is for your extended service to me."

Holmes took out a guinea and flipped it to the started boy, who stared at it in amazement.

"A GOLD piece? For MEEEE? Thank you, Mr. Homes, thank you!

The lad ran from the room and bounded down the stairs as though the devil himself was after him. Mrs. Hudson happened to be in the hallway and gave him a yell as he flew by out into the street. In a moment, all was quiet again.

"I believe I shall have Wiggins recruit him into the ranks of the Baker Street Irregulars. Such a brave lad will go far, Watson."

The doctor remained unimpressed. "But what did we learn from his report? He noticed nothing and no one out of the ordinary, other than that mystery woman. You don't believe that Sir Henry would be taken in a second time, do you, Holmes? Could this be the other possible conspirator that you are worried about?"

"Watson, you know my opinion of women. However, in this case, I am positive that Sir Henry is under no threat THIS time. Use my methods. Can you not analyze the facts? Take them one at a time—she is not from the village, she is more than likely shunned by the elders of Grimpen, and she was a young woman alone at the festival. Does that not bring someone to mind? It should, you know, for we have already met her."

Watson beamed. "By Jove, Holmes; it's Laura Lyons! But what does it mean?"

"For one thing, it means that Sir Henry is not letting the grass grow under his feet, Watson. Good for the baronet. He may be more resilient that I gave him credit for. But more importantly, it would appear at the moment that my fears about a missing confederate of Stapleton's are unfounded."

"I'm glad to hear it, Holmes. Does this mean that you will now help Lestrade with that business of the broken Napoleons?"

"All in good time, Watson, all in good time. For the present, let us finish our now cold breakfast or Mrs. Hudson will be offended."

CHAPTER 6

A Short Trip

"I must say, James, the Palace of Hollyroodhouse was absolutely stunning. I had heard descriptions from friends and acquaintances, but I could not appreciate its beauty until actually seeing it with my own eyes."

"I must agree, Henry. It was actually built about four hundred years ago, adjacent to an old Augustinian abbey. There is rich history, both good and bad associated with it, as it is with most grand structures of power; but Edinburgh is all the more noted for it, I can assure you."

The two men walked side by side along a narrow, cobblestoned street that stretched out ahead of them, while compact buildings of wood and stone flanked them on either side as the sun began its descent. A quick look down the even narrower side streets gave one the feeling that these areas were not quite safe to walk through. Dr. Mortimer smiled as he glanced at Henry straining his neck to see around a bend in one of them.

"For your information, that is called a close," as he pointed down an alleyway.

Henry laughed. "I can see why. A man could certainly feel claustrophobic ambling down one of them. I certainly would not care to attempt such a journey in the evening, I can assure you."

"They provide the quickest route on foot to New Town, if your business is THAT important. Now for a short walk. All of this, my friend, is known as the Royal Mile. It starts at the palace to Canongate, then goes to High Street, the Lawnmarket, along the Esplanade, and finally to Edinburgh Castle."

Henry looked up and marveled at the strategic military importance of their destination.

"I am certain one can look out and see for miles all round, James. It had to be virtually impossible for an enemy to sneak up unawares. And it appears quite the imposing fortress."

"That it is; I believe the fort has been attacked over a dozen times. It was built on a volcanic crag that is known hereabouts as Castle Rock. Of course, a structure as old as this morphs over time as it is adapted to the changes in military tactics and fire-power, but I suspect that the old fort has damn near run its course."

"What else can we expect to see once we get inside?"

"Well, one of my favorite haunts is what is referred to as the Crown Room, where the crown, scepter, and sword of Scotland are housed. And speaking of haunts, if we are fortunate, we may come upon the Bald Agnes."

"BALD AGNES? Who is she, may I ask?"

Mortimer chuckled. "She's the ghost of a woman who was tortured and stripped naked after being accused of witchcraft a few hundred years ago. She is supposed to haunt the castle."

Sir Henry turned pale and did not answer. The doctor became angry with himself.

"I am very sorry, Henry. I should not have brought up the subject. We are here on this trip for you to regain your strength and composure. Forgive my foolishness."

"That's quite all right, James. I AM feeling a bit better, since you mentioned it. The change in scenery has done me good. It's just that sometimes…in my dreams…I'm alone at night on the moor and I look back to see the hound bounding towards me with its red eyes and open mouth; then I wake up shaking and feel weak all over again. I…I guess it's going to take some time to un-jumble my nerves, that's all."

Henry appeared embarrassed by the sudden confession, but the doctor chose to ignore his friend's plight.

"Yes, of course; time is just the tonic you need, old boy. Now let's pick up the pace a bit so I can be sure to show you St. Margaret's Chapel. It's the oldest building in the castle. Off we go."

Unbeknownst to them, while Henry Baskerville and James Mortimer were starting their trek up the Royal Mile, Jack Stapleton was emerging stone faced in the dusk from the Grimpen Mire. Forced to live much like the animal he had housed in the abandoned tin mine, he was hell bent on revenge.

With nothing but time on his hands, he had devised new schemes to rid the world of his cousin, and anyone else who was foolish enough to have offered the baronet assistance. But that was not the immediate problem. He had seen Henry and the good doctor leaving Baskerville Hall in the estate carriage stacked with suitcases. That could only signal a trip; but to where, and for how long?

He could not possibly wait them out under his present circumstances; the living conditions were appallingly primitive. No, he had to gain their attention AND force them back to Dartmoor without delay. Fortunately, Merripit House provided him with the means to do both.

It was only a short wait before darkness fell over the moor. This was the hour for Stapleton to wend his way past jagged tors and unforgiving bogs, finally moving on a parallel course just off line with the dirt roads to his home. He stayed back behind the stone wall and surveyed the area for several minutes, anxiously looking for a light or some sign of movement.

When he was satisfied that the house was deserted, he crept up to the back door and unlocked it without a sound. Walking through the first floor to his study, he drew a match and candle from his pocket and proceeded to light it, placing it carefully on his work desk. The illumination revealed small corked bottles, tubes, and a microscope. Jack Stapleton was now one with his new instruments of death. All of the bottles were labelled, and to all intents and purposes appeared quite harmless. But it was the combination of the ingredients that would prove deadly.

"The idiot police could not see what was in front of their own eyes" he chortled with great amusement. "This will prove to be much more effective than the hound, and with little effort expended on my part."

He set about gathering his ingredients with relish. In an alabaster bowl, he painstakingly began to mix the elements of liquid forms of nitrogen, hydrogen, and finally, carbon. When Stapleton had close to forty cc's of his concoction, he got up for a moment and ventured to one of the many specimen collections he had amassed while hunting out on the moor.

Spying one in particular, he removed it from the framing with a tweezers and gently placed it in the bowl with care and with as much distance from his own body as possible. Allowing the liquid to envelop and absorb into it thoroughly, he laid the specimen into a tiny wooden box and then placed that in the pocket of his overcoat with a final pat of reassurance. Once he had looked around the room to make sure he had left no evidence of his presence, a quick pinch of his fingers snuffed out the candle and plunged the room back into total darkness.

Stapleton exited out the back door of the house and locked it once again. Now it was on to deliver the item that would most certainly bring Sir Henry back to Baskerville Hall, and to the moor. It was dark enough now for him to walk on the roads without being seen. This would cut down the journey consider-ably in terms of time.

Within the hour he was standing directly in front of the home of Dr. Mortimer. He could see Mrs. Mortimer and a maid conversing in the downstairs parlor. That was good. Stapleton knew the layout of the house, having been a dinner guest on numerous occasions in the past. After a quick trot around the back he was climbing the sturdy vines growing over the stone exterior, finally reaching the second floor and the master bed-room.

With a great effort he opened a window just a crack. He could only use one hand; the other was grasping the vines to keep him from falling. He reached into his coat and placed the wooden box on the outside sill, then again used the tweezers in his pocket to position the specimen on the inside portion of the sill. All was in readiness.

After climbing back down, Stapleton stood patiently behind a tree in full view of the bedroom window. He did not have long to wait. The lights on the first floor were extin-guished, and he noticed the flickering of a candle as it illumi-nated the bedroom and its occupant. Mrs. Mortimer shortly began her night time ritual for bed, but soon stopped and went directly to the partially opened window.

Her figure blocked out the light, leaving only a silhouette, but he could see that she had bent over slightly then picked up the object on the sill, cupping it gently in both hands and bring-ing it close to her face for inspection. Stapleton could not have asked for a finer performance from his unsuspecting neighbor. It was simply a matter of time now.

Time—that was a commodity that Sir Henry and his com-panion guide thought they had plenty of. Continuing their trip through Scotland, they made stops at Glasgow, Inverness, and the Northern Highlands, ending up in Thurso on the shores of Pentland Firth. There they sat in their hotel dining room having supper and discussing the next move.

Henry looked closely at his plate of haggis before taking a knife and fork to it. "So, James, tell me about these Orkney Islands. You say that one of your cousins actually lived on one of them?"

"One of my wife's cousins, to be exact. He and his family lived on the largest of them all, which is appropriately called Mainland. There are somewhere in the neighborhood of seventy or so islands in all. There is a stone circle near the Lock of Horray, and we can also investigate another one called the Ring of Brogdar that is thousands of years old. But the crown jewel of them all could very well turn out to be Skara Brae, a partially uncovered Neolithic stone village just off the Bay of Skaill on Mainland's western coast. It should remind you of the structures on our own moor back in England."

"Well, then, I shall look forward to seeing it tomorrow. James... there is a page coming toward us with a letter."

The words had no sooner left Sir Henry's lips than a young boy smartly dressed in a bellhop's gray uniform and cap anxiously sidled up to their table.

"Excuse me, sirs, would one of you by chance be Dr. Mortimer?"

James looked surprised for a moment, and then his expression quickly changed to an air of concern.

"Yes, my boy, I am Dr. Mortimer. What is it?"

"A message from Dartmoor, sir; it's marked urgent"

The doctor snatched the envelope and tore it open. The message was short, but from the movement of James' eyes the baronet could see that he was reading it over and over again, as though not fully comprehending the meaning.

"Something is wrong, James. What is it?"

Mortimer dropped the paper on the table and stared at his friend in disbelief.

"It says that my wife is...DEAD! She fell ill quite suddenly and died last night. The authorities have been trying to trace us since then. I must get...back. Oh, Henry, she died and I was not even at her side! How could such a thing have happened? She was in perfect health; no current sickness, no illness from the past. I simply cannot believe that my Catherine is dead...yet it is so. What am I to do, Henry? What am I to do?"

Baskerville reached over and placed a hand on his friend's shoulder, pressing it gently.

"You are to go up to your room and pack for Dartmoor immediately, while I make train reservations at the front desk. One of the hansoms outside can take us directly to the station, where I can wire the authorities in Grimpen of our impending arrival. I shall then have Perkins waiting for us at Okehampton. With any luck, we can be back in a day."

Mortimer was unimpressed as he lowered his head slowly. "With any...luck? I can say for certain that word no longer has any meaning for me."

While Henry was able to make all necessary connections and personal contacts in a flurry of activity, James became morose and slow to act on the return trip. Conversation between the two became virtually non-existent. The doctor merely stared out of the window without noticing the scenery. Occasionally, he would mutter some words that Henry could not make out, but the baronet was sure that his friend was remembering some happy past events with his late wife, and wisely let them pass without a remark.

The baronet was true to his word. Within twenty four hours, their final train connection pulled in at Okehampton Station at dusk, where Perkins was waiting with the Baskerville coach. Sir Henry and Perkins spoke in low tones as Mortimer climbed inside and took a seat.

"Shall I take Dr. Mortimer back to his home, Sir Henry?"

"No, that's the last place he should be right now, Perkins. Take us directly to the hall. The doctor shall overnight with me, and then we will start fresh in the morning. There is much to be done. After you drop us off, go to the authorities in Grimpen; inform them of our arrival, and relay that we shall meet them at the police station in the morning. Have you made inquiries about the…body?"

"Yes, Sir Henry. It is presently at Williams' Mortuary. The body has been made ready for transport. The Mortimer family housekeeper helped with the preparations; you know…the dress and all."

"I understand. Now let us be off. There is much to be done."

A final, silent ride ensued to Baskerville Hall. Passing through Grimpen on the way, Sir Henry noticed a strangely dressed individual on horseback waiting at a crossroads. As the carriage passed, the baronet saw the man look up and wave to Perkins in the driver's seat, then quickly ride off into the darkness. He thought it an odd occurrence, but his thoughts were broken by Dr. Mortimer.

"Where are we now, Henry?"

"On the way to the hall, remember? You're staying with me tonight, and in the morning we shall go to the authorities to find out what…information we can."

"Yes, quite right. Thank you, Henry. You've been a great help to me. I don't know how I can…."

"And don't forget that you've been a great help to ME ALSO. If you had not contacted Mr. Holmes when you did, I would not be here with you now. Ahh, we have arrived."

Perkins slowed the coach to a crawl, and finally to a complete stop in front of the main path to the hall. The Barrymores were waiting patiently outside like stone lions to greet their master and retrieve the baggage. The butler spoke first.

"Welcome home, Sir Henry. It is good to have you back with us."

"Thank you, Barrymore. Perkins will help you with the baggage. Mrs. Barrymore, has a room been prepared for Dr. Mortimer?"

"Yes, Sir Henry, along with a late supper, if you and the doctor are hungry."

"I believe that we will take you up on your proposal. What do you say, James?"

The doctor looked at Henry with a blank expression. "If…you insist…I suppose I could use some food."

"Excellent; then let us go inside and out of this damp night air."

As the Barrymores took some of the baggage into the hall, followed closely by Dr. Mortimer, Sir Henry laid back to speak to the driver.

"Perkins, who was the man on horseback that waived to you? I don't recall having seen him before."

"Why Sir Henry, that was Murphy, the gypsy horse dealer. He was the one out on the moor near the hall the night your uncle was …died. He heard Sir Charles scream, but could do nothing. I thought that was odd, since the moor is usually quiet and the fog hangs onto any sound that is made."

"Thank you, Barrymore. You can bring in the rest of the baggage later. You'd best get to Grimpen and speak with the police. Inform them that we shall arrive by mid-morning."

A quiet night proved to be no help for Dr. Mortimer. He looked exhausted as he appeared in the dining room for breakfast with Sir Henry. It was obvious that he had slept very little, and his interest in the hearty servings from Mrs. Barrymore was virtually non-existent. The baronet knew he would have a difficult task full trying to keep his friend's health from deteriorating any further. Barrymore finally broke the silence of the meal with his arrival into the dining room.

"Sir Henry, Perkins has informed me that the carriage is ready."

The worried baronet glanced across the table at his guest before speaking. "It is time we are off to confer with the authorities, James. They will be waiting for us. Are you ready?"

The doctor let out a sigh. "Yes, let us see what we can learn from their...investigation. I understand that Catherine is at the mortuary, ready to be brought home for the wake."

"Yes, Perkins made the transport arrangements after conferring with the police. Your housekeeper is also making preparations for later on."

The short ride to the Grimpen Post Office and Gaol was uneventful, but as the doctor emerged from the carriage, Henry saw a noticeable change in his friend's demeanor. The depression was gone, replaced by a steely determination. Villagers who recognized James as they ventured in and out of the building deferred to him out of respect, with the men removing their hats.

The two men opened the front door and stepped inside the bustling room; all conversation inside ceased. A constable sitting behind his desk finally broke the silence as they stepped forward.

"Good morning, Sir Henry. Dr. Mortimer, my condolences. Please follow me to the back if you will. Sergeant Bullfinch is the man you want to see. He is in charge of the investigation."

Led by the constable, the trio stepped into the back hallway and made their way into the same room that Laura Lyons had been a prisoner not too long ago. The irony was not lost on Sir Henry. Behind a desk was a large, barrel-chested policeman with a set of sergeant's stripes on his uniform sleeves. The man recognized Mortimer at once and rose to shake his hand.

"My sincere condolences, doctor. I wish that we could have met again under better circumstances." Bullfinch turned to the baronet to explain. "The good doctor tended to my little one not too long ago; a first rate job."

Mortimer perked up for an instant. "And how is little Sally getting along after her episode with the mumps?"

"Right as rain, doctor, thanks to you." There was a long pause, and the sergeant's voice became melancholy. "Sad business, this death, gentlemen…sad business."

The doctor nodded slightly to acknowledge the man's sympathy, and then spoke. "Sergeant, I understand that it was my housekeeper Anna who first discovered the…my wife, is that not correct?"

"Yes it is, doctor. She stated in her deposition that she went up to the master bedroom that morning, as your wife hadn't come down for breakfast, and when the door was opened she found her lying dead on the floor. Mrs. Mortimer was in her night gown, but the bed had not been slept in. The covers were not turned down."

He went on. "Anna found Mrs. Mortimer lying on her back with her mouth and eyes open, and her right hand clutching her chest. Her face was a bit flushed. It was clearly a heart attack, I'm sorry to say, but it was evidently quick, if that's…any consolation to you, doctor. Once I sealed off the house I sent for the county coroner. It took him some time to get there, with the distance and him being so old and all, but after his examination, he confirmed what I had suspected."

Sir Henry interrupted. "Then he did not perform an autopsy?"

Bullfinch shook his head from side to side. "We didn't see the need. There were no signs of forced entry or a struggle, and Dr. Bates has seen a hundred heart attacks in his day, so he thought it best not to..." the sergeant glanced at Mortimer, "go through with the ah... procedure, sir, seeing as how it was Dr. Mortimer's wife."

Mortimer had been standing all the while with his eyes closed, quietly taking in the information. He pursed his lips for a moment, then opened his eyes and spoke.

"Thank you, sergeant. I am quite satisfied that everything was done properly. If you would excuse us, I must go directly to the mortuary to conclude final transport arrangements to my home."

CHAPTER 7

The Unknown Accomplice

Sir Henry quickened his leisurely pace when he finally caught sight of the home of Dr. Mortimer in the distance. He noticed a large man waving at him from in front of the house, but he could not quite make out who it was. When the baronet got within shouting range, he was able to discern that it was Sergeant Bullfinch from the police station. The sergeant was out of uniform and dressed in a noticeably cheap dark suit, but this Baskerville was not impressed by mere appearances.

"Ah, sergeant, it was good of you come and to pay your last respects to Mrs. Mortimer. I am sure that the good doctor appreciates your gesture."

Henry then glanced around the front and sides of the house and displayed a quizzical look. "With the exception of Reverend Musgrave's, I don't see any carts or horses from the neighboring farms. Has no one else arrived yet? The daylight is just now starting to fade. I don't quite understand."

The sergeant appeared embarrassed by the question while shifting his feet back and forth. After a moment's pause he shook his head slowly and replied in a soft tone.

"I regret to say I don't think there's anyone else coming, Sir Henry...except for those few already inside."

The baronet thundered. "NO ONE ELSE COMING? THIS IS OUTRAGEOUS! What could possible keep the neighbors and villagers at home at a time like this?"

Bullfinch replied soberly "Fear... plain and simple, Sir Henry."

"FEAR? Fear of WHAT, for heaven's sake?"

The sergeant took a deep breath and explained. "Well, Mrs. Mortimer was in perfect health, you see, Sir Henry, so the thought of her up and dying from a heart attack does not sit well with the folk hereabouts."

The baronet tried to quell his mounting anger. "And what do they THINK she died of, then?"

"That's the fly in the ointment. They just don't know, so they're staying clear, sir, kind of like a precaution if you will. More than that, I honestly can't tell you. Don't be too hard on them, Sir Henry. People around here are a superstitious lot. It goes hand in hand with all of those ghostly stories about the moor, sir."

The baronet was not sympathetic. "If not for the memory of my Uncle Charles, I would withdraw my support for the civic improvements and tell them all to go to blazes. Now I must go inside and see my friend. By the way...I notice that fear has not kept YOU away, sergeant."

Bullfinch gave off a thin smile. "As I mentioned before, Sir Henry, Dr. Mortimer tended to my little girl when she was ill. I'll not be forgetting that."

The two men shook hands and Henry made his way down the path to the partially opened front door, which was draped in black crepe. He took off his hat and coat, then stepped inside the hallway, where he was met immediately by the Mortimers' housekeeper, Anna. Her eyes were noticeably red from crying. She said nothing but pointed to the study.

The baronet stepped silently into the room and looked about. There were only a handful of people besides the grieving widower; Mayor Sexton, Mr. Frankland, Reverend Musgrave, and the reverend's housekeeper, Mrs. Beale. No one from Grimpen or the outlying farms was anywhere to be seen, although the room was filled to overflowing with funeral bouquets of all shapes and sizes.

The flowers were clearly sent by neighbors and villagers whose fear of the woman's untimely death kept them from actually attending the wake in person. However, Sir Henry's anger was not dampened by the ostentatious display spread out before him. He began to mutter under his breath and pursed his lips together. Reverend Musgrave seemed to sense the baronet's displeasure and came over to him at once, putting a hand on his shoulder.

"Don't judge these people so harshly, Sir Henry. I've known them for many years, and they are good and honest folk. It's just that...old habits and customs die hard, even in OUR new age. Look over there on the mantle, for instance; do you notice anything strange about that clock?"

Henry stared for several seconds before responding. "Other than the fact that it is almost nine hours off the mark, no, I see nothing of significance."

The vicar smiled. "It is not off the mark, as you say, but stopped altogether. It was deliberately stopped once Mrs. Mortimer was brought into the house."

The baronet was incredulous. "But WHY for heaven's sake?"

"Ahh, there we have it, because if you do not stop the clock in a death room you will have bad luck. I assume that was done by Anna, who was merely performing a kindly service for Mr. Mortimer. Do you notice anything else that you might consider an oddity?"

"The wall pictures are not on their hangers. They are all on the floor, facing outward and angled backwards. Don't tell me…"

"Yes, another superstition; it has been said that should a picture accidentally fall off a wall, then someone you know will die. In our particular case, it would be one of the people here in this room. NOW perhaps you can begin to understand what we are up against. All in all though, these are harmless trappings, Sir Henry. You have seen something of the enlightened world, been afforded a good education, and so on. Go easy on my parishioners, and please do not think unkindly of them."

The baronet softened. "I begin to understand…a little, reverend. Thank you for the information. Now if you would excuse me, I must go and pay my respects."

The room was quiet and filled with the scent of the floral sprays, most of which were placed on and around the closed mahogany coffin of Mrs. Mortimer. In the middle was a framed photograph of her nestled over the coffin, with the words "AT PEACE" spelled out in red and white roses underneath the picture. Her husband was staring at it intently when the baronet approached and touched his elbow in an effort not to startle him. The widower was the first to speak.

"Henry! I appreciate the visit. Thanks so much for coming so see me…and Catherine." The baronet was touched by his friend's admission, but also slightly embarrassed.

"James, to tell the truth, I am lucky to have made it here at ALL. I decided to walk from Baskerville Hall, so I instructed Perkins to bring the carriage around to pick me up early in the evening. Well, I was walking along on the main path, and was just in the process of passing one of the higher tors when a section of its top sheared off and tumbled down in my direction, nearly crushing me. It was all I could do to get out of the way of the boulders rushing down on me."

Mortimer was stunned. "That's a bit of bad luck, although it is common for granite to shave off like that, Henry. You don't know which one it was?"

"Unfortunately, James, I'm not a local, so these tor names are completely foreign to me. However, I will ask Perkins when we pass by it on our return to the hall. If that had happened to someone like…Mr. Frankland, for instance, I'm sure he would have been killed." A voice answered the baronet's statement; it was none other than Frankland himself.

"That would certainly have been unfortunate for me, gentlemen, since I have had a recent run of good luck with my law suits. Some of the Fernworthy residents are presently up in arms about my latest triumph, closing the woods where they used to intrude and picnic, leaving trash all about. In truth, had I been crushed by a landslide, one could almost make a case for murder, would you not say? I have succeeded in angering a great many people."

Mortimer gave him a pained look. Sir Henry, sensing the miscue, turned in the direction of a woman who had just entered. She was standing by herself in a corner. Frankland quickly realized that he committed a grievous breach of social etiquette and began to stammer out an apology. The baronet did not wait to hear it; he made his way hastily to the new arrival.

"Well Laura, I am glad to see that there are some with the courage to do what is right. It was good of you to come. I am sure that James greatly appreciates your presence here tonight."

Her reply surprised him. "I could not stay away. Dr. Mortimer has been supportive of me concerning my matrimonial situation. He stood by me, a stranger, when I needed help, and now, I am here to help him. I consider this more of a duty than a debt."

The baronet was impressed with her keen sense of objectivity, and her inner strength made him admire her. "I see. You did this, even knowing that you would most certainly come face to face with…your father?"

Laura was unperturbed. "He will ignore me now, as he has done in the past, but I do not care. I go where I choose. It is MY life."

Sir Henry understood that there was more to this woman than met the eye. She was a person of strong will and character, and he found himself being drawn to her despite the present morbid circumstances. As they stood smiling at one another, Mr. Frankland caught sight of the daughter he held in disgrace and attempted to make a hasty retreat to an adjoining room with as much dignity as he could muster. The baronet was annoyed by the obvious intended slight.

"I see that your father has decided to maintain his position towards you, Laura. That is HIS loss. May I once again offer you safe passage home in my carriage? Unless my hearing has failed me, I believe Perkins is just now pulling up to the front of the house."

Laura beamed; "I would be happy to accept your invitation once again, Henry. You do realize that this will infuriate my father, do you not? He wishes me to remain an outcast to society."

"I will frustrate him on both accounts, if I have my way," Henry stated wryly as they expressed their final condolences to the good doctor and left the house together. Perkins was initially surprised as he opened the carriage door for his additional passenger, but he recovered quickly and was up in the driver's seat before the pair could begin a conversation. He turned the carriage around in the trifling light of a waxing crescent moon, unaware that something was trying to keep pace with them off the side of the road all the way to the outskirts of Coombe Tracy.

On another part of the moor, a man was waiting patiently at the gloomy outer edge of the great Grimpen Mire. He had been there since dusk, pacing ever so deliberately back and forth with his hands in his coat pockets in an effort to keep the late autumn weather from chilling him to the bone. There was no thought to making a fire.

Even the moor's bush crickets became indifferent to his cadence and sang out to one another through the darkness. That sound was the stranger's alarm system. Unable to see more than a few yards, he depended heavily on the moor's indigenous inhabitants to alert him of an impending arrival, and he was not to be disappointed.

He sensed that he detected slow and deliberate footfalls coming towards him from the direction of the morass, so he remained motionless as the sounds increased. Shortly thereafter, the crickets ceased their chirping altogether, and the decisive moment was at hand. Jack Stapleton emerged from the deadly mire with several empty jugs. As he passed close by the stranger without notice, the quiet one announced his presence in a low, even tone.

"I KNEW you were still alive, Mr. Stapleton."

Jack recognized the voice in the darkness, and rather than turning in alarm to confront an enemy, he drew near and returned the acknowledgment with great enthusiasm.

"MURPHY! We meet again at LAST! You're certainly a sight for sore eyes. It's been torturous out here, I can assure you. What was it that led you to believe that I had not been killed?"

The gypsy chuckled. "When the police could not find you around Dartmoor, they simply assumed that you had died crossing the morass in panic. The fools did not know what I knew, that Jack Stapleton could find his way blindfolded through all that hellish muck to any damn spot he wanted on the Grimpen Mire. I'd stake my own life on it. Even that bastard outsider Sherlock Holmes was taken in by their story. It was a convenient one for them...gave the police an excuse for not actually capturing you."

Stapleton was ecstatic. "Excellent, Murphy; excellent! I see that my faith in choosing you as a partner in all this was well founded after all. Now we shall go to Merripit House. I must have more fresh water."

Murphy put up his hand. "There's no need for that, sir. I knew you would be needing supplies, and brought provisions with me."

With that, he turned and picked up two bulging haversacks, one of which he handed to Stapleton. Although the gypsy could not possibly see, the murderer's eyes glistened with appreciation.

"Your stake in this little scheme of mine has just now increased, my friend. I know how to compensate those who serve me well."

Murphy grinned in anticipation. "And just how MUCH of an increase are you proposing to give me? I have endangered myself a great deal on your behalf already; great risk calls for great rewards."

"I will give you that coward of a servant Antonio's share in addition to your own. I believe that should keep you comfortable for quite some time. Now what do you say to that?"

The gypsy was less than enthusiastic. He knew that his associate was in a vulnerable position, and needed to rely heavily upon him for aid. This was a situation that demanded full leverage, and he was prepared to take full advantage. He replied with a triumphant sneer.

"The circumstances have CHANGED, Mr. Stapleton. Before I was merely a lookout and would help tend to the hound with Antonio. NOW I am your eyes, your ears...your last hope for success, one could argue. Do you not agree?"

Stapleton was briefly taken aback by the sheer impudence of this gypsy, a mere seller of horse flesh who was shunned by his own kind from a makeshift wagon community out on the moor. After all that he had accomplished and endured, the thought of being at this man's mercy was almost too much to bear. The anger of Sir Hugo swelled within him like a raging fire, but he quelled it just enough to buy himself some time. His voice was calm, almost melodic in its short response, something that Murphy failed to notice.

"And just how many pounds do YOU think would be a suitable reward for your services in this…continuing endeavor?"

Murphy's face hardened as he inched closer. "I no longer desire a SUM of money. What I want is a percentage of the estate after we dispose of Sir Henry. After all, we ARE talking about a number of murders that are punishable by death. My neck can be stretched as easily as yours."

Stapleton retained his composure, but now the words were nearly spitting out of his mouth. "And just how much of a percentage do YOU think is a fair bargain?"

The gypsy paused for a moment and gave off a false look of compassion which was immediately perceived by his cohort. "I deserve…a 40% share."

Stapleton's eyebrows rose at the very thought of such an arrangement, but he felt it best not to provide an immediate response. No, he would leave Murphy in doubt for a while, perhaps making him believe he had overplayed his hand. He turned and began walking back into the mire.

"It's not safe for us to be talking about such things, even out here on the moor. Come back with me to the mine where we can discuss a plan of action. I will walk slowly; follow close behind me and be certain to step where I step, do you understand?"

Travelling through the Grimpen Mire at night was a nightmare that no local would wish on his worst enemy, but Murphy was compelled by his own greed to do as instructed. Stapleton was true to his word and carefully led the gypsy through a meandering labyrinth that spelled certain disaster with one false step. He was counting on the constant fear of slow death to help suppress his companion's sudden sense of superiority, and it worked to perfection.

When they finally arrived at the entrance to the mine, Murphy's nerves were stretched to the breaking point. Despite the coolness of the evening, he was sweating profusely and breathing through his mouth with short, choppy pants. He began to squeal. "How much longer do we have to go, and how can you possibly know to stay on the hidden path?" He had obviously reached his limit.

Stapleton was pleased with the sound of fear from Murphy. "We are here now" he responded in a soothing voice as he stopped in his tracks and waived him on. "Come and see for yourself."

The gypsy took a few shaky steps forward and stared at a small crag. It was unassuming enough, even attractive, with pink and white heather surrounding a hole in its center the size of a double door. "This is the mine?" It was not what he expected.

"Yes," replied Stapleton, "and a perfect place to hide. The natural vegetation has grown back over the years and covered over most of the entrance. Remember, it was abandoned years ago."

He bent over and picked up an oil lamp hidden beneath the brush. With a strike of a match, the welcome glow of light rose from the lamp and brightened their shadowy world. Murphy let out a sigh of relief as his shoulders dropped. "That's more like it."

Stapleton lowered his head and waved away some of the heather as he entered the mouth of the mine with the lamp illuminating the shaft. "Now in we go." Murphy followed close behind, but what he observed once inside raised his fears once more.

Rubble was everywhere, causing him to lose his balance with each step. The height and width of the shaft was not much greater than five feet, causing him to feel claustrophobic. Timbers propped up the dripping jagged ceiling at regular intervals, but several appeared to contain dry rot. Even the rail tracks were rusted clear through in sections. It was not a place that a prudent man would venture, at least not very far.

But the most striking element was the odor that permeated the mine. The brackish water seeping from the mire and the dust that permeated the air gave off a foul stench that caused the gypsy to gag. Stapleton was up ahead but he could still hear the gypsy's suffering, not that it concerned him to any great extent.

Murphy could wait no longer. "Just how far down are we going into this filthy hole?"

Stapleton's reply was icy but reassuring. "This filthy hole, as YOU call it, is now my home, thanks to the meddling of Mr. Sherlock Holmes. We need only go around the next bend to make sure that the light does not escape out the mouth of the mine. Ahh, here we are."

Blankets lay stretched out on the dirt floor, while articles of clothing were draped over a small wooden freight wagon still sitting on the rail tracks. Stapleton began to empty his haversack and place the items inside the wagon. He motioned for Murphy to do likewise.

"These corfs have come in quite handy. In this one I've stored all of my necessary items, while another further down the shaft holds my trash. No need to give away the fact that someone inhabits this place.

Now, Mr. Murphy, there is much to discuss. Events have transpired that you need knowledge of if we are to complete our unfinished task. And now that we have been reunited, as it were, we can move on to bigger and better things. I still believe that the use of the hound was a stroke of genius. The very idea of a supernatural element in the Baskerville deaths was something that I cannot hope to duplicate."

Murphy suddenly regained his composure and puffed up his chest with no small measure of pride. "But I can, and not only that, it will be GENUINE. You will not believe what I am about to tell you."

CHAPTER 8

Death By Association

The old gentleman was nestled comfortably in a high back Windsor chair with his elbows cushioned above the arm rests. A large tankard filled with brown beer was situated in the middle of the table in front of him. He reveled in the darkened atmosphere of the pub, which made it difficult for him to be seen by the rest of the customers, but in no way impaired his own vision. This was HIS personal table in the corner, reserved just for him.

It was early evening, and there was no better place in all of Westmoreland to perceive how a person's day had just unfolded. Locals stood draped over the red oak horseshoe bar chatting affably amongst themselves, while the smell of roast venison mixed in quite nicely with the aroma of the swirling cloud of tobacco smoke wafting up towards the wooden raftered ceiling. Yes, this was a special place.

A middle aged man entered carrying a valise. He was obviously a traveler, but he stood waiting in the doorway, as though expecting to be noticed. The gentleman was not disappointed. The bartender looked his way and gave out a cry of recognition, while another fellow at the end of the bar smiled and came towards the new arrival with his hand outstretched.

The three men huddled together exchanging stories for some time when the bartender pointed in the direction of the old gent. The traveler's mouth opened wide, and then he made a mad dash towards the darkened corner of the room. He stopped in front of the table and gawked for several seconds before speaking.

"Well bless my soul. It's…James Desmond! Hawkins said that you were here, but I couldn't half believe it. I have to say that you're a ghost right out of the past, deacon. It must be what…nearly 30 years gone by. I suppose you don't remember ME, do you sir?"

The old man's eyes glistened with delight while he took a sip of his beer, and then he smiled up at his excited inquirer.

"OF COURSE I remember you, MASTER Sean Condon. What manner of teacher does not remember the names and faces of his own students! Please have a seat."

Condon was flabbergasted but thoroughly delighted that he had not been forgotten by his favorite childhood instructor. He sat down quickly, as though he was afraid the invitation would be suddenly rescinded. Now it was his turn to smile.

"I have to admit that I AM surprised that you remember me, sir. You were the only private tutor who could make the subject of Latin interesting."

Desmond gave him a sideward glance and decided to test his old protégé. "All right, then, we'll see about that. Let us see how good of a teacher I REALLY was. Recite for me the gladiators salute."

Condon stood up and raised his right hand in a fist at a forty five degree angle in front of him before speaking. "Hail Caesar! Those who are about to die salute you!"

The deacon was unimpressed, and he quickly waved him off as though shooing a bothersome housefly. "No, no, no. I don't give a hoot about the English translation; give it to me in Latin Sean, in Latin."

Now came the moment of truth. Condon hesitated for several seconds, and then beamed with recollection. "I've got it! Here goes: Ave, Caesar! Morituri te salutant!"

Desmond took a long swig from his tankard. "EXCEL-LENT! MOST EXCELLENT! I knew you could do it, my boy. Here's to you...but you aren't a boy any more, are you? What brings you back to Westmoreland after all these years Sean?"

"I've come home for the marriage of my sister's eldest son, and then I must be on my way once again. Hawkins wrote to me that you had retired from the church and decided to settle in town. Are you far from here?"

"Bless my soul no; actually, I'm just a block or so down the road, which is a good thing, because I believe I've had a little too much to drink tonight. Sean, could you possibly consider giving me a hand, so to speak? I broke my hip a few years back and I have trouble walking, especially when I'm a bit tipsy.

It was a slip and fall that lead to my self-imposed retirement from the church. You see, I was unable to make my rounds; you know, to visit the sick, the needy, and those in search of spiritual guidance. At the end, the vicar could not even entrust me to help pass out communion. Yes, it was a sad time, but...all things happen for a reason, they say. It is God's will."

"Sir, it would be my honor to escort you home. Say your goodbyes to everyone here and we can be off."

The unlikely pair soon made their way out of the pub, Desmond shuffling slowly and rocking from side to side, while poor Condon watched nervously, ready to pounce should his childhood teacher lose his balance. It was a pleasant walk for old Desmond; he chattered away about old times and parishioners long gone, but the end of the journey could not come soon enough for his companion, who felt he bore a great responsibility to the wonderful old man whom everyone had grown to love.

It was the longest short walk that Condon ever took, and they arrived at a modest, pleasant looking cottage at the end of a narrow lane. The gas lamp in front of the house was not on, which seemed unusual as all of the others on the street were fully functional and burning brightly. Up to that particular point they had kept the darkness at bay. This made for a some-what dim atmosphere that blended in well with the misty rain that began to fall.

Condon took the deacon by the elbow and walked him up the stone steps to his front door. He was greatly relieved that he had escorted him home in one piece. It would not have been a pleasant remembrance had an accident occurred.

"Well, sir, here we are, safe and sound. I daresay that you will sleep soundly tonight."

Desmond laughed heartily as he stood in the open door-way. "I certainly will do that, Sean. I would invite you in, but as you can see, in my present condition, I think it best if I went straight to bed. I do appreciate your assistance, and I am VERY happy to have chanced upon you once again. Nothing gives me greater pleasure than seeing my former students and parish-ioners. And now that you know where I live, I would expect you to call upon me the next time you are in the vicinity."

"You have my word on it, sir. Good night and God bless you."

As Sean Condon made his way back towards the pub to reminisce with old friends, the deacon closed the door behind him and stepped out of the foyer to light an ornate gas wall lamp. He gently turned a knob at its base and a low hiss could be faintly heard. Next came the strike of a match against the wall, and he zigzagged the tiny flame with an unsteady hand towards the center of the lamp. In an instant the sconce gave out with a poof and light flickered onto the first floor's

surroundings. The old man mumbled a heartfelt "Thank good-
ness."

He was quite pleased with his progress thus far. The walk
home was uneventful, he could see where he was going, and
now all that was left between him and a warm feather bed was
a flight of stairs. Unfortunately, he did not have the where-
withal to notice that an adjacent stained glass window in the living room had several of its paneled panes broken, and its lower
sash was forced up.

The clergyman's confidence got the better of him, and he
attempted to take off his clothes while climbing the steps, stopping about half way up to unravel himself from his uncoopera-
tive slicker. He had barely reached the top step when a figure
darted out from the hallway and grabbed the old man by the
lapels. With one firm shove, he thrust Desmond backwards.

There was nothing the poor man could say or do. His back
and head fell against the unforgiving wooden stairs with a loud
thud, and momentum simply did the rest. His feet flew over
him with a sharp spinning motion, and he continued down like
a rolling stone, until he lay in a tangled heap in the middle of
the hallway. A shrill gasp escaped his lips, and all was silent in
the house once more.

The unknown assailant waited at the top of the stairs for
several seconds, and then descended swiftly to check on the sta-
tus of his victim. There was no movement to the chest, and the
eyes gazed vacantly into space, while a gaping mouth revealed
split lips and several freshly broken teeth. The killer proceeded
to rummage through Desmond's pockets, turning them inside
out, then he went to the door and opened it ever so slightly to
peek outside.

The gas street lamp that he had disabled just an hour or so
before gave him a warm feeling of safety. He looked and listened, but for the exception of a yapping dog across the street,
there was no sound, and more importantly, no one in sight. He

slipped outside and softly closed the door behind him. Raising the hood of his cloak over his head, he turned to his right and headed out of town; thus ended the life of the beloved James Desmond.

But the town of Westmoreland would not be the only locale to note the sudden passing of the well-respected clergy-man. Back on Dartmoor, a nervous Sir Henry would get word of his cousin's untimely death but kept the news to himself. Now, several days after the funeral for his friend's wife and the arrival of the London engineers to inspect the old, damaged bridges in the area, the baronet sat at the head of the dinner table in Baskerville Hall, flanked on either side by James Mortimer and Laura Lyons. Mrs. Barrymore brought out dessert, while her husband carried a sterling silver pot of coffee.

Despite his recent loss, the doctor was making a concerted effort to remain upbeat during the evening's dinner party. He did not want to spoil the first formal visit by Mr. Frankland's estranged daughter. Normally, Laura's place at the table would have been taken by her father, but as a result of his own intran-sigence and pride, having the pair together in one room was completely out of the question.

Mortimer spoke up. "I must admit that it feels good to be back here at the hall, Henry. It has been a while since we've dined together in your home. Thank you for inviting me."

"You need no invitation, James, not do you need to offer advance notice should you wish to dine with me at ANY time of the day. So how are things REALLY going with you?"

"As well as can be expected, my friend; fortunately, I have my practice to attend to, and it has kept me quite busy as of late. There has been a mini epidemic of chicken pox in the area, and both adults and children have been affected. I realize that we're not talking about the black plague, but I HAVE been bouncing continuously from house to house, both in Grimpen and on the moor. It has been quite exhausting, really."

Laura chimed in. "James, I have heard nothing of that sort going on in Coombe Tracey, but if I do, I will be sure to notify you at once. Our local physician is much too old to go traipsing about the countryside. I fear that if he did so he might need a doctor himself, or worse for that matter."

The three of them laughed almost in chorus, but Henry and the doctor noted her compassion and concern for others, even those who had ostracized her as a result of her current atypical situation. It was a trait that was particularly valued by the baronet.

"It's like you to care about even those who think ill of you merely because of convention and custom, Laura. It is their loss, and if I may be so bold…that loss should be most keenly felt by your father, who is a BLASTED FOOL!"

Mortimer watched as Laura blushed while her eyes gave off a gleam of appreciation, and perhaps something more. Henry stared at her thoughtfully for several seconds, and then his face softened with a smile. The doctor could sense that there was a bond forming between these two individuals, and he was very much in favor of it. He decided that now was the time to make a prudent farewell.

"Thank you all for a splendid evening, but I must be going. I fear I shall be busy again tomorrow, and I will need as much sleep as I can muster. This pox has yet to run its full course. Laura, it was a pleasure to see you once again. Henry, I believe that the next dinner invitation should come from me. I shall notify you BOTH."

Perkins brought Mortimer's trap around to the front of the hall, and heartfelt goodbyes were exchanged by all. The couple stood staring silently as the doctor veered around a bend and was out of sight. Finally, Laura broke the stillness.

"Henry, there is something I need to talk to you about, now that James has departed. May we retire to the library?"

The baronet let out a laugh, and replied as though pretending to be affronted. "Wait a moment; that is something meant to be spoken by the MAN of the house to his male guests when he wishes to offer them brandy and cigars. WOMEN don't venture into LIBRARY, my dear lady."

The reply was short and sweet, befitting Laura's views and temperament. "Poppycock, Henry Baskerville. This is something important. Now will you escort me to the library or not?"

Mrs. Barrymore was in the dining room cleaning up and inadvertently overhead the brief conversation. It was all she could do to contain herself from dropping the dishes. She immediately ran back into the kitchen to tell her husband, whom she was sure would not believe her.

Henry extended his right arm to Laura, and she gently took it as they made their way into the Victorian era's inner sanctum sanctorum. Both felt totally at ease with the other, and they wondered how such a beautiful thing had happened so quickly. When they reached the library, Laura sat in a plush burgundy leather arm chair on one side of the fireplace, while Henry occupied its twin on the other. He waited respectfully for her to begin the discussion. Her features became tense, and her words came out with great difficulty, as though she did not want to say them at all.

"Henry, this may sound strange…but I sense something ominous is hovering over you here on the moor, almost as though something or someone is secretly watching and waiting. I felt its presence the day I walked to the wake of Mrs. Mortimer, and I haven't been able to get the feeling out of my head ever since. Of course, you may simply judge me a silly woman for bringing it up, but I had to let you know how I felt."

The baronet sat back in his chair and exhaled quietly as he stared into the fireplace, then gave her an odd look. He had thought Laura was going to question him about any legal leverage that his solicitors in London had been able to make use of pertaining to her desired divorce. This however, was a completely different matter, and he was caught off guard, but it was one that he was happy she had brought up.

"How funny that you should mention it, Laura; I thought that my imagination was playing tricks on me, but…I too have felt uneasy of late. I can't put my finger on it, and I can't really describe it, but it's there nevertheless. So you have felt the same way too; how interesting."

Laura shot upright in her chair. "INTERESTING is not a word that I would use to call this, Henry. I believe that your LIFE may be in peril once more. Would you do me the favor of…writing to Mr. Holmes and asking for his advice on the matter? He has a very perceptive mind, and as he has already been out here on the moor, I would feel more comfortable if he were aware of our joint concerns."

The baronet nodded in agreement. "If that is what you wish, my dear. I highly value your judgment. Unfortunately, there is more to this than a mere ominous sense of foreboding, as you so succinctly put it. Certain events have…well, I promise to write to Mr. Holmes tonight, and the letter can be posted in the morning. Does that assuage your trepidation?"

"Only for the moment, Henry, because now I am certain that there are other things you have kept from me…to shield me, but I'm sure you have your reasons, and I won't press you. Would you ask Perkins to bring the carriage around? It is time I left for home."

In a few minutes the couple found themselves standing outside the front door, waiting and looking into each other's eyes, saying nothing. Finally, Henry leaned forward and kissed Laura gently on the cheek. They believed that their actions went unnoticed, but that was not the case. Just outside the limits of the hall lights on the front lane, they were being watched with a great deal of curiosity.

Upon Laura's departure, Henry stayed true to his word; he went directly to the study and sat down at his desk. Barrymore came in quickly thereafter with a tray and a snifter of brandy on it, placed it down next to the writing table with a smile, and left without so much as a word. After taking a sip, the baronet took pen and paper in hand, sitting quietly for a few moments to gather his thoughts; then, he began to write.

Dear Mr. Holmes,

I hope this letter finds you and Dr. Watson well and in good health. I realize that it is not even a month since you left the harshness of the moor to return to the comforts of London and Baker Street, but there is much to tell, and it appears that I am in need of your help and advice once again. I fancy that one could make the case that I have merely stumbled into a string of unfortunate events, but I shall recount them and let you be the judge.

The first incident occurred on the way to the Grimpen Fall Festival. My carriage lost a wheel going round a sharp bend in the road, and it was only by the blessings of Providence that I was not crushed to death. Perkins, our driver whom you have previously met, has sworn to me that he checked the carriage for any sign of trouble that very afternoon, and there were no visible defects of any kind. I trust him. Of course, he could have simply overlooked the imminent problem, but I don't believe that to be the case.

The second event took place when I was walking alone on Dartmoor. As I passed a high tor whose base terminates by the edge of the road, a large portion of the upper granite facing sheared off from the main section and tumbled swiftly down upon me like an avalanche. Fortunately, the rumbling gave me a precious second of advance warning, and I was able to dive out of the way to safety, with only my pride injured. Of course, that sort of thing does happen now and again on the moor, but I found it extremely unlucky, or should I say extremely strange, that it should occur just as I was passing by?

The third episode is one that I hesitated to relate to you, since it did not involve my well-being directly, but is of so strange a nature that I feel compelled to tell you. You were previously aware of my plan to go on an extended holiday with Dr. Mortimer to calm my nerves.

That did in fact take place, but while we were in Scotland, James received word that his beloved wife Catherine had died suddenly. Mr. Holmes, I swear to you that the woman was in perfect health, and yet the coroner's report stated that she had died of a heart attack. James tells me that there is no previous history of heart failure in her family, so what are we to make of this?

Finally, I must relate a very recent death in my family, my cousin James Desmond of Westmoreland, who as you well know was next in line in the event of my demise. I am sure that you are thinking it should not come as a shock due to his advanced years. However, he did not die of natural causes. The poor man was beaten to death in his own house by a burglar. The police believe that James came home and chanced upon the scoundrel while he was in the process of searching the house for valuables. The old man could hardly have posed any sort of threat to the rogue, and yet he was killed nonetheless in a most violent way. The local newspaper in Westmoreland, The Herald Statesman, stated that it was the first murder in that community in over 20 years.

Mr. Holmes, I am not an alarmist by any stretch of the imagination. One or even possibly two of the above incidents within the short period of time since you left Dartmoor could well be argued to be merely a case of bad luck. But all four appear to me to be a palpable threat, but from what I do not know. Laura Lyons, a brave and sensible woman who has become a good friend and confidant, thinks very much as I do. In fact, it was she who advised me to write to you in the first place.

I have made the decision to come to London as soon as possible to confer with you and Dr. Watson about the aforementioned events. I shall check the train schedule forthwith and be in the city sometime the day after tomorrow. When I arrive, I shall go directly to the Northumberland Hotel and contact you from that location. In the meantime, please make use of the time and contemplate my unusual situation. Although I hope it is not the case, it would appear that I have need of your services once again.

Sincerely,

Henry Baskerville

CHAPTER 9

Off To London

"Henry, I would like you to send me a telegram after you have conferred with Mr. Homes and Dr. Watson. Will you do that for me?"

The baronet smiled as he took Laura's hands in his while the coach rattled noisily along the road towards the station. There was more than sentiment involved when he asked her to accompany him to the train, and he wanted to make sure that no one else would be able to overhear their conversation.

"Of course, my dear; to be honest, I would have done so without your asking me. But before I leave Dartmoor, I wanted to tell you something very important, and it concerns the two of us."

Laura gave off a quick look of surprise at the cryptic statement. She stared at him for several seconds, waiting for the squire to reveal his secret. His face was purposely blank and he said nothing; it was then that she nearly jumped out of her seat.

"Oh, Henry! You have heard from your solicitors in London! Is it good news? PLEASE tell me!"

"Yes, it is good news. We have finally located Mr. Lyons, but I must confess that using the word mister before his surname is not a sign of respect but rather of formality. He is presently residing in Cardiff, and fortunately for us both, he has taken to gaming as well as drinking, and as such, he is in a poor state of monetary affairs, I can assure you. My solicitors have…persuaded him to grant your release from the marriage."

Laura could not quite comprehend what had just been spoken. After a long pause, she burst into tears and covered her face with her hands. Long sobs followed, and the baronet wisely did nothing. He waited patiently for her to compose herself, knowing that the weight of the world had just been lifted from her shoulders. This was the harsh legal existence for women in the age of Queen Victoria.

Finally, she took several deep breaths, wiped her eyes, and looked up at him with sincere appreciation before speaking up. "Tell me, Henry, how were you able to DO this?"

"My people used the law to YOUR advantage this time, Laura. The wheels of justice turn slowly at times, my dear, particularly when changes weaken those in power, who in this case would be the male of the species in general. You were undoubtedly unaware, as was I, of the Matrimonial Causes Act of 1857, which made the civil courts the governing body responsible for granting divorces for women rather than relying on an act of Parliament. Your husband counted on this quite heavily, and I am sure purposely gave you misleading information on the subject."

Laura let out a melancholy sigh and shook her head in affirmation. Sir Henry went on hastily, trying to get through the details as quickly as possible.

"However, unfortunately for him, my solicitors dug much deeper into the law. It states the courts may mandate that a husband pay maintenance to an estranged wife. Since you are both living apart AND under acrimonious circumstances, my solicitors simply demanded what was your rightful due, including payment of back funds commencing when the two of you began living apart.

Fortunately for us, he can barely fend for himself, let alone care for your own well-being. He has been given the option of fulfilling his obligations under the law, or agreeing to a divorce. Your husband has wisely chosen the latter. It is only a matter of a few weeks now, my dear, and you shall be a lady free to follow your own path, and I ask that path leads you to... Baskerville Hall."

"Oh, Henry, you KNOW that is my wish! I feel as though I have awakened from a long and terrible nightmare. But what about the people of Dartmoor? What will they think of a baronet marrying..." she looked away..."a DIVORCED woman?"

"I have neither the time nor the inclination to concern myself with their social prejudices. But I am completely confident that when they begin to know you as I have, you shall be accepted with open arms, and hearts. If we give them time, the rest will...what the devil is THAT?"

Sir Henry had become distracted by some sort of movement out the carriage window. He brushed aside the curtains to get a better look, but whatever was out there had gone.

Laura became concerned. "What was it Henry? What did you see?"

"I...I really don't know, my dear. I thought I noticed something like a moor pony keeping pace with the carriage out of the corner of my eye. No matter, it seems to have disappeared, and we are arriving at Oakhampton Station."

Perkins pulled the carriage to the side of the road and waited for the baronet's call. He was a quiet and unassuming man but an astute judge of circumstance.

"Perkins will take you back to Coombe Tracey, Laura. I will write to you as soon as I have conferred with Mr. Holmes and we have decided upon a course of action, if any. In the meantime, try not to worry."

Henry leaned forward and kissed Laura on the lips. At first, she thought of pulling back, still being a married woman, but her feelings got the better of her and she returned the momentary affection. He had wanted to do that for some time now.

"All right, Perkins. I am ready now." The driver gave off a thin smile and bounded down with his master's suitcase as they made their way into the station house.

"Have a safe trip, Sir Henry, and please hurry back to us."

"Thank you Perkins. I will try to...Perkins, did you happen to notice anything unusual out on the moor while driving me here?"

"Well, now that you mention it, Sir Henry, one of those moor dogs, and a particularly big one at that, followed us for several miles until we reached the outskirts of Oakhampton. That's most likely my fault. The wife packed a lunch for me for the way back, you see, and the beast probably picked up the scent of the meat is all. It's a hard life for those dogs that have wandered away from their owners and gone wild, particularly for that one, I expect."

"Why do you say so?"

"This one was limping badly. Under the circumstances, I mean without proper medical attention...that amounts to a slow and painful death sentence from starvation. Here comes your train, Sir Henry, and I wish you a pleasant stay in London."

Upon boarding the train, the squire saw to the delivery of his baggage to a first class compartment, and then went directly to the dining car for lunch. He was seated by a white jacketed steward, who laid the menu on the table as though presenting an original Shakespeare manuscript. The bill of fare was not as dear: Pork Chops, Poached Eggs, Steak and Kidney Pudding, along with Bread and Cheese. The baronet scanned the list without much enthusiasm and eventually decided on the pork chops. It was then that his mind somehow wandered back to the poor dog on the moor.

While Henry Baskerville was glancing over the dining car menu, Sherlock Holmes stood staring out the window in his Baker Street lodgings. He held Sir Henry's letter in one hand, his calabash in the other, and he was utterly lost in thought. Watson pretended not to notice as he thumbed through the London Times, and he made sure to make an abundance of rustling noise with the newspaper. Finally, when he came to the realization that the sound would not distract his friend from his contemplations, the good doctor could stand it no longer.

"Odd's fish, Holmes, are you going to tell me what and why Sir Henry has written to you so soon after the hound affair? My first inclination was that he was merely sending you his regards from some interesting locale while on his holiday, but your actions say otherwise. What exactly is going on?"

The great detective snapped out of his musings and turned towards the doctor with an uneasy look. "I wish I knew, Watson. Look this over for yourself and give me your opinion on the matter."

Holmes watched intently as his colleague from many previous cases read the letter with the utmost care. Finally, after a long minute of silence, Watson cleared his throat and spoke quietly but deliberately.

"If Sir Henry is implying that there are evil forces still at work attempting to murder him, I must say that I fear for his very reason, Holmes. The man's nerves were badly frayed by the affair. These are nothing more than a series of unfortunate accidents and misfortunes. I hope that you're not seriously entertaining the notion that the case that I have called the Hound of the Baskervilles is yet unresolved. Why…it's ridiculous!"

"You think so, Watson? Consider what has transpired since our departure. Let us take these misfortunes as you call them one at a time. First his carriage loses a wheel."

"Holmes, that carriage has been in the Baskerville family for many years. It is well past its prime."

"Then what of the avalanche when Sir Henry just happened to be passing by?"

"A strange happenstance, yes, but not an uncommon one; tor rockslides do take place naturally, and Sir Henry saw fit not to look for a man made cause for it."

"And what about the sudden death of Mrs. Mortimer?"

"Heart failure can take place even in the healthiest looking people. It happens every day. Modern medicine has much more to learn in this particular arena, I regret to say."

"Well, what do you make of the murder of James Desmond? That old soul wouldn't harm a fly."

"The poor man was in the wrong place at the wrong time, Holmes. He happened upon a burglar in his own house, and in the dark the scoundrel didn't realize how frail his victim was."

"BRAVO, Watson! I must congratulate you on a most thoughtful series of explanations."

"Why, thank you, Holmes. It's kind of you to..."

"Unfortunately, you are COMPLETELY mistaken."

Watson's shoulders drooped when the unexpected words of his friend had sunk in. Holmes took no notice. He clapped his hands together and began pacing back and forth in front of the fireplace with a look of great concentration.

"Now let me tell you what I think of all this. We shall start in reverse order with James Desmond. The well-known deacon was as poor as a church mouse, yet a burglar picks that man's modest house to rob AND then kills the old gentleman to boot. No, Watson, that won't do. It is more likely that he was killed because he was next in line to the Baskerville fortune in the event of Sir Henry's death."

"Holmes, you're not back to that again! I can't believe..."

"Then there is the sudden death of Mrs. Mortimer. What better way to cut short Sir Henry's holiday and get him back to Dartmoor than to murder the wife of his own travelling companion?"

"How could you think that, Holmes? You have no proof; no proof at all. Why, it's preposterous."

"Preposterous, is it? We shall see about that. And finally, there are the TWO sudden and mysterious accidents that very nearly cost Sir Henry his life. When you add all that up, it smells of cold, calculating murder, Watson. This case is NOT closed. I should have heeded my instincts. If you are an honest man, you will make sure that this blunder is brought to light along with my successes that you so fervently chronicle."

The doctor was stunned. "Great Scott, Holmes! You... you may be right. But what do we do now."

"Now? We shall wait to hear from Sir Henry once he arrives in London and takes rooms at the hotel. When we receive his communication, we shall go there directly and explain to him that he is still in great danger. This is MY fault, Watson, and I must not allow any harm to come to this man. He is the last of the Baskervilles."

As Holmes and Watson waited impatiently in their lodgings, the baronet walked confidently into the luxurious atrium of the Northumberland Hotel and made directly for the front desk. The manager was arrogantly giving detailed instructions to a weary clerk situated behind the counter, but when he turned to meet this new guest, his face turned pale. In a flash, he blubbered out a salutation.

"Oh my God. It's you...I mean...welcome back to the Northumberland, Sir Henry. We are honored that you chose to sojourn once again at our hotel while you visit London."

The squire was taken back for a moment, but then he recalled the circumstances of his previous stay, and was even faintly amused by the situation. He also recalled that he did not care for the manager, so he decided to make the best of this situation and bring him down a peg.

"Ahhh, yes, you are Mr....Thompson, are you not?"

"Why yes, Sir Henry; how kind of you to remember. One of our FINEST suites has been reserved for your stay and..."

Sir Henry drew near. "Mr. Thompson, I hope that there will not be a duplication of the chain of events that plagued me during my previous stay in your establishment."

The man looked as though he were about to faint, much to the delight of the clerk and bellboy waiting to care for the baggage. "I assure you that will not be the case THIS time, Sir Henry. The employee who stole your boots has been discharged."

The baronet feigned indifference. "That's all well and good. Now, to the present. It is getting late, so I will dine here in the hotel, but first, I would like to send a communication to a certain house on Baker Street. Can that be arranged?"

"Absolutely; we here at the Northumberland pride ourselves on total service to our customers. Clarence, some note paper and a pen, and you, boy, take these bags to Suite 378. Now if you will excuse me, Sir Henry, I must attend to our other guests."

Mr. Thompson made a hasty retreat while on a high note of efficiency. He was certain that if the squire encountered a problem on THIS trip, he would most certainly be the NEXT employee to be sacked. Sir Henry smiled as he watched the manager take flight, and then turned his attention to scripting the letter.

Dear Mr. Holmes,

It is now 6PM and I have arrived at the Northumberland. I shall have supper in the hotel and then stop by your lodgings. I trust that you and Dr. Watson have had time to consider my previous letter conveying the strange circumstances that have plagued me in recent days. I wish you to be frank with me in this regard, and I will abide by any conclusion or plan of action that you deem appropriate. Until then.

Sincerely,

Henry Baskerville

While the squire was finishing his meal in the dining room, a lethargic, heavy set young page ambled up to the entrance of 221B Baker Street. He rang the bell twice and was shortly thereafter met by Mrs. Hudson, who admitted him to the boarding house, read the name on the envelope, and pointed up the stairs to the first door on the right.

The lad trudged up the stairs in a sweat with great effort and knocked loudly on the door. Moments later, it opened and he presented a letter to Watson. As the doctor's family was originally from Scotland, the page was given a trifling gratuity and left more miserable than when he had arrived. Watson casually turned to his friend.

"I believe this is the communication that you have been waiting for from Sir Henry. Do you..."

In one motion, Holmes dashed forward, snatched the letter from the startled doctor's hand, and tore it open to read its contents. Watson could sense that something had gone wrong. "What is it, Holmes? Is it from young Baskerville or not?

"Yes it is, but Sir Henry states that he is coming HERE tonight to confer with us. He is not safe on the streets of London, Watson.

Our only hope is that Sir Henry decides to take a hansom to Baker Street. If he were to walk instead, I fear that his life would be forfeit. Come, we haven't a moment to lose."

As the pair raced out of the boarding house, the baronet emerged from the hotel and pondered his next course of action. The wind picked up, and a slight drizzle caused him to shudder. Just then, he heard a voice from the street. It was a hansom cab driver waiting for his next fare. The man's face was mostly hidden by his hat pulled low and coat lapels turned up, but it was of little significance to the squire when he called out.

"Ello guvnor. Can I interests you in a ride? The night's gettin' a chill on, it is."

Sir Henry looked up and then paused for a moment before answering. "Actually, I've just had a fine meal and I think a walk would help my digestion; thank you anyway, my good man. But perhaps you can help me in another way. I'm no longer that familiar with London. Baker Street is off to the left, is it not?"

The cabbie appeared reluctant to answer at first. Sir Henry thought it was merely due to the fact that the man had just lost a possible fare. "Yes it is; go down four blocks and then makes a right onto Baker Street. A blind cat couldn't miss it."

The words were hardly spoken when the baronet began strolling to his appointment. The driver was correct in one sense. The night had begun to turn foul, and there were few pedestrians going about their business. The squire took no notice that the cab kept pace with him about 10 meters behind.

Finally, as Sir Henry stepped off a curb and found himself half way across the entrance to a side street, the hansom thundered up and blocked his path. Two men jumped out and tackled the baronet before he had the chance to let out a shout for help. They wrestled about on the ground, with the muggers punching away furiously, while Sir Henry attempted in vain to get to his feet.

Then, out of the corner of his eye, the baronet spied the glimmer of a knife, and he began to lose hope, but just as one of them was about to bring the blade down upon him, his hand felt a loose cobblestone in the roadbed. He picked it up and swung wildly into the face of his oncoming assailant, who fell backwards onto his companion.

Just then the driver gave out a shrill whistle, a signal that danger was approaching. The two ruffians dashed off back into the hansom, which then turned in a wild semi-circle and sped away in the opposite direction. All that could be heard was the sound of fast approaching footsteps. The exhausted squire waited patiently to gaze upon his deliverers, and when he did, he was not surprised.

"Mr. Holmes! Dr. Watson! Over here. It appears that you have saved me once again. I seem to have been a prime candidate for a robbery; serves me right too, for not paying attention. This is not Dartmoor, I am afraid."

He swayed for a moment, and then Holmes reached out to steady him. "You are safe for the moment, Sir Henry. Our lodgings are close by. Dr. Watson can better care for you there; come with us."

In a short while they were back at 221B with the squire slumped in a chair. The doctor hovered over him, cleaning dirt from numerous cuts and scratches to his face and head. "You've taken a terrific beating, my boy. I fear the possibility of a concussion."

His patient gave out a sharp laugh. "I believe a concussion is the least of my troubles, doctor. Could you please look to my right side…over here? I am having trouble breathing, and fear that something is broken."

Watson pressed his hand gently on the spot where he was directed, and the baronet jumped in his chair. "Sir Henry, you are no physician, but you are right on the money. You have a cracked rib, possibly several. I can give your outer chest cavity a tight bandage wrap, but other than that, I am afraid that only rest and time can heal your injury. You will have to deal with some degree of pain I daresay."

Holmes came away from the window and stood before his battered guest. "Well, Sir Henry, I believe we no longer need to debate whether or not your life is still in danger. Obviously, you were to be murdered tonight, and your death staged to look as though it was a robbery gone badly, just as it was in the case of your unfortunate cousin, James Desmond."

The squire was not convinced. "How can you be so sure in THIS instance, Mr. Holmes? Perhaps the blaggards…"

"Did they ever demand money, or give you any opportunity to hand over your valuables?"

"Why…no. They attacked without as much as a word."

"It would have been less risky for your adversary to have you die in London than back at Dartmoor, Sir Henry. Your misgivings have proven to be correct; the loose wheel, the crashing rocks, your cousin, all were part of an ongoing plot to eliminate you."

Sir Henry agreed, but with little enthusiasm. "The nightmare goes on then. But what of Mrs. Mortimer?

Holmes answered the question with a touch of sadness. "You must see the bitter truth of it now, Sir Henry. James's innocent wife was obviously murdered to force you back to Baskerville Hall, where you could be watched and ultimately struck down when the time was right."

"But Catherine died in her own bedroom of heart failure. Both the local police and coroner attested to it at the inquest. Surely THAT is mere conjecture on your part."

Watson chimed in sternly with his hands on the lapels of his suit jacket. "If I have learned one thing from working with Holmes over the years, Sir Henry, it is that he does NOT make rash statements."

Holmes smiled briefly to see his friend come so quickly to his defense. "Despite Dr. Watson's obvious bias in this instance, he also happens to be quite correct. I am sure that we will get to the bottom of THAT mystery once we have returned to Dartmoor."

The squire perked up. "So you WILL return with me, gentlemen? I say, that is certainly a weight off my shoulders. I feel safer already. But...who is trying to murder me NOW? The hound is dead, along with Jack, its master. His wife Beryl is in a London prison and the servant Antonio is long gone from the region, most probably all the way back to Costa Rica. Who else could possibly want me out the way?"

Watson shrugged his shoulders and looked inquisitively at Holmes, who shook his head slowly in reply. "THAT is what we shall discover upon our return. There is, of course, any number of people who may fit into this narrative, although their motives may be shrouded from us for the moment."

Sir Henry sat up in his chair with concern. "Just who do you mean, Mr. Holmes?"

"I mean possibly those people whom we have already met, although I daresay there may be some characters still hidden from us. There are your servants the Barrymore's, who harbored a fugitive behind your back; your neighbor Mr. Frankland, who enjoys litigating those about him and kept his daughter's existence from you; even your new friend Laura Lyons must be included as a suspect, I am forced to declare. Remember, it was HER letter that caused your uncle to be out late on the grounds that night of his death."

The baronet's face grew red, and he attempted to stand up, but his injury prevented him. He winced in pain and promptly sat back down in a huff. However, he was emphatic in his reply. "Mr. Holmes, I DO NOT agree with your last statement, sir, and furthermore, I find the accusation insulting both to Mrs. Lyons and myself. The utter..."

Watson spoke up quietly. "Sir Henry, I regret to bring up the fact that you most probably felt that same way about Mrs. Stapleton not too long ago. I believe in your heart you must know this to be true."

Sir Henry stared at the floor and sighed, then raised his head. "Of course, you are right, doctor. I apologize for my out-burst gentlemen. I know that you are both looking out for my well-being. Nevertheless...Mr. Holmes, I would stake my life on the integrity of Mrs. Lyons. I can safely say that she is NOT a suspect."

Holmes stared hard and long into the eyes of the squire. "I hope for your OWN sake, Sir Henry, that you are correct."

CHAPTER 10

The Vixen Tor Witch

M urphy the horse trader took a deep breath and stepped
out of the shadows into the gypsy encampment. Nothing had changed since he had lasted visited; in fact, not much
had changed in years. The wagons belched smoke from the
roofs with their iron pipe chimneys, women sat close to bub-
bling cauldrons of food hung over fires that dotted the perimeter and men stood in small groups speaking softly to one
another.

The sweet sound of a violin echoed above it all, giving off a
peculiar soothing effect. But that was soon to change. As soon
as Murphy was observed, the music stopped. One of the men
approached him menacingly, trying to control his anger. The
others turned their backs; some women shooed away the children while others stared into their fires pretending not to notice.

Finally, the angry gypsy spoke up.

"What are you doing here? Do you have horses to sell? If
you do, be quick about it and be gone. You know you are no
longer wanted in our camp."

Murphy was stone faced in his reply. "Luca, I am not here
for that. I will sell horses tomorrow at the crossroad as I always
do. I have another reason for my visit. I wish to see…Syeira."

A hush settled over the camp, as though the name itself was evil. Murphy snorted. "So, you still fear her I see. Do not worry. I am not here to curse any of you, but tell me where she is and be quick about it."

Luca wavered and pointed to the wagon that was the farthest away. "She has not come out for several days. Perhaps she is dead"... then his voice trailed off..."if we are fortunate."

Murphy laughed. "I will tell her of your wish; until tomorrow then." He strode off in the direction of the far wagon. By the time he reached it, the camp was deserted. All others had retreated to the safety of their own wagons, the fires still burning bright.

A low, throaty voice answered Murphy's knock. "Enter, it is unlocked." He climbed up the short set of wooden stairs, opened the door and stepped inside. It was just as he had remembered. Brightly colored shawls were spread out over the walls, while the floor was covered with a thick brown rug to keep out the cold.

A stove was off in a corner giving off a good supply of heat, and a well-lit oil lamp hung from the center of the ceiling. An old woman sat on a crate behind a small round table topped with an assortment of odd trinkets and herbs. She smiled affectionately at Murphy.

"So, Nicola, you have come to visit with me again I see. You had no trouble this time with the others?"

Murphy's face soured. "Nothing to speak of. They are all fools."

"They still harbor bad feeling against you and yours. When your mother left us years ago to marry and live with that gadjo in the village, they felt betrayed, and it is never a good thing to betray a gypsy. And yet, she did school you in our ways, but not enough for you to return to us after their deaths."

She leaned forward in her seat and looked into Murphy's eyes. "So, my grandson, HAVE you decided to come back, or are you here for the OTHER reason?"

He was quick to answer. "It is for the other reason that we spoke of. I need that power to reach my goal."

Syeira cocked her head. "Then let me explain to you fully. Raising the dead is a deed filled with peril. It is usually done to bring back loved ones who have passed, but YOUR motives may be even more dangerous, especially for the one you seek. I know that as a child you had heard bits and pieces from your mother as a way to keep you from straying far from her, but shall I tell you the whole story, and how the cursed one met her end?"

Murphy provided no reply, but he also did not object, so Syeira continued. "Her name was Vixiana. According to our legends, she lived hundreds of years ago and was a gypsy witch who was driven from her camp. This act enraged her, so she sought vengeance against any person who happened to cross her path. She lived in a cave at the base of a high tor on the moor.

The gypsies and locals knew well enough to stay away from the area, but strangers and lost travelers died horribly at her hands. You see there was a deep bog near her tor just off the main trail. She would stand on the tor scanning the countryside night and day for victims. When an unfortunate ventured close, she would summon a thick fog to blind the person, and then call out directions for a safe passage.

But she was in fact luring the poor souls to their deaths. Her instructions led straight into the bog. Once the screams would begin, she would clear away the fog to watch the person struggle in terror and agony as the filthy muck slowly sucked the traveler down into its depths. This went on for many years, as there were only whispers of the "Witch on the Tor," but travelers continued to disappear.

Finally, two brothers, noblemen adventurers and brave of heart, decided to put an end to the district's shame. They ventured out and searched each and every spot on the moor, until they finally came upon Vixiana in the distance, as they could see her standing on top of her tor. They split up, one acting as bait, staying on the path while the other made his way around in a circle to catch her by surprise.

When she saw a figure approaching, she sent out her fog and it covered the path, but this time, the stranger ignored her directions. The other silently climbed the back of the tor until he was right behind her. Vixiana could not understand why there were no screams, so she leaned over and blew away the fog with a wave of her hand. That was the moment the other brother pushed her off and into the bog, where she herself met the same horrible end as so many of her victims. You know of that spot today as…Vixen Tor."

Murphy reacted with surprise. "Yes, I DO know the site. At a certain angle, the tor gives off the face of an old woman. THAT is the location of this witch? The bog is still present…so she must still be at the bottom of it."

"That is correct. You should also know that the one who resurrects the dead gains the power of control over them; but although you have not seen fit to tell me your motives, I fear that you will use this power for an evil purpose. I can only counsel you to put aside your plans."

Murphy shook his head. "It is too late for that. I have already made up my mind; besides, my future benefactor has sworn me a handsome reward that will allow me to live in comfort for years to come. I cannot pull back now."

Syeira sighed and went about the room gathering objects from shelves and drawers, which she placed dutifully in particular order on the table. Murphy appeared puzzled by the proceedings but said nothing. Finally, when she was content with the configurations, she addressed him confidently.

"Here I have five bowls; the blue one represents water, the white one air, the red one fire, the green one earth, and the clear one...spirit. These are all of the elements in the eternal circle of life. You will also see that they are placed as a pentagram to provide protection. In each of these bowls I place salt, the symbol of perpetual obligation. The birch twigs I crumble and place in each one represents new beginnings and female energy."

Syeira then reached into her pocket and produced a match, which she lit to set each of the bowls on fire. The flash and subsequent smell was much like church incense, but in a sickly sweet sort of way. After the fires tapered off, she poured a clear liquid on each one and produced a heady smoke that filled the room.

Murphy asked "Is that only water?"

Syeira responded with a foul giggle. "It is HOLY water stolen from a church font. I require it for many of my...rituals. Take each of these and pour them on the spot where the person is buried, then read the bit of parchment within this tortoise shell amulet...and the deed is done. Always keep the amulet around your neck with this sliver of grapevine. Now take it."

"I cannot thank you enough for your help, grandmother."

Syeira was unmoved. "You may not give thanks after what you plan to do. Remember the tortoise shell. It shields the wearer again her."

While Nicola Murphy gazed upon the rite of resurrection, Sherlock Holmes stood facing a roaring fire in the great room of Baskerville Hall with his hands outstretched in an effort to gather some warmth. Watson sat in a large, comfortable chair not far away wrapped with a blanket around his shoulders. A half empty glass of brandy was on a nearby end table. The detective was performing his due diligence.

"So, Barrymore, I understand that you originally planned to leave Sir Henry's employ once he had made other arrangements.

The sudden death of Sir Charles struck a chord with you and your wife did it not?"

"Why yes, sir. We truly loved Sir Charles, and did not believe at the time that we could remain at ease here. However, Sir Henry's kindness in the no small matter of Selden, my brother in law, changed our minds. And once you solved the murder, we felt it was our duty to remain, so to speak. After all, my family has served the Baskervilles for well over a century, living in the south wing all the while. Why, we feel that we are a part of the hall, too, sir."

Holmes raised an eyebrow but said nothing. Watson noticed the change and spoke up. "Thank you, Barrymore. Are our rooms prepared? It is getting late and we have had a long travel day from London, particularly Sir Henry. His ribs are giving him trouble I am afraid. The ride from the rail station in the trap jostled him more than we feared. I have wrapped his chest as tightly as I possibly can, but there is a limit."

"I believe they are nearly prepared, doctor. Eliza, my wife, was just finishing tidying them up. I will check at once, sir. Excuse me."

The pair watched and waited until Barrymore had left the great room, then they looked at one another. Holmes was the first to speak.

"So they consider themselves part of the hall, do they? What do you make of that statement, Watson? Perhaps he is a hidden accomplice that we seek."

The doctor was not convinced. "I know where you're heading with this, Holmes, but I find it hard to believe that the Barrymores would plot against the one family that provides them with a rather comfortable employment situation, and can do so for years to come."

Holmes was unimpressed. "Nevertheless, we know for a fact that Barrymore sent a nightly signal to Selden out on the moor for food and clothing. He admitted to it, and he was caught in the act. But what if that was only a half truth?"

Watson blinked in confusion. "Half-truth? What do you mean, Holmes?

The detective moved towards his friend and returned the question. "What if Selden was not the ONLY person that Barrymore was signaling to upon Sir Henry's arrival to the hall? What if he was also signaling to...Jack Stapleton? In his will Sir Charles had left the couple one thousand pounds. Would not Stapleton offer them much more if they could help him to become the last living Baskerville?"

Watson stiffened in his chair. "Great Scott, Holmes! I never thought of that. So you believe..."

Holmes quickly cut him off. "I believe nothing, Watson. I am merely formulating a possible theory. Time will tell us many things. Fortunately, we are now here on site to guard Sir Henry. The important.."

Holmes stopped speaking as Mrs. Barrymore entered. "Your rooms are ready gentlemen. Please follow me. I trust that you will sleep well."

As they followed Eliza up the broad beamed stairs to the second floor landing, Holmes turned back to Watson and whispered. "I wonder what foul mischief is taking place out on the moor this very night."

He was so right. Several miles away in the darkness, Jack Stapleton and Nicola Murphy had arrived at the base of Vixen Tor. They stood silently in front of an ominous bog that lay before them with fear and dreadful anticipation. There was no going back now.

"All right, Mr. Stapleton; empty the contents of the bowls into the bog one by one while I read from the parchment, and then make sure that you get behind me. Do you understand?"

Jack was brusque in his reply. He did not like the idea of his partner having the upper hand in such a dangerous situation. "Yes, yes; I'm starting. Let's get on with it, damn you."

Murphy reached for the amulet that hung about his neck, and then turned the shell over to reveal the words on the parchment. Even though he had the spell memorized, he still felt it necessary to have it directly in front of him. He moved a lamp near to his face and read the rhyme with a quivering voice.

"Gatekeeper: Free this creature from endless night. Raise it up to see the light. Let its heart no more be still. Then bend this being to my will."

At first, nothing happened. They stared into the greenish brown muck as though mesmerized, their faint breathing the only sounds to be heard. Then a large, fist sized bubble belched up over the surface, followed by several others smaller ones. What liquid there was began to swirl and lap back and forth.

Finally, a claw like hand appeared, followed by a head and torso. The creature flailed wildly about until it reached firm ground and pulled itself out of the bog. The men could scarcely believe what had just transpired as the sputtering witch coughed up mud and tried desperately to catch a welcome breathe of fresh air.

Once that was accomplished, she straightened up her reeking, dripping form and slowly opened her eyes. They were still filled with the burning hatred of centuries gone by. Stapleton stepped back instinctively, while Murphy let out a sharp scream that alerted her to their presence. She jerked her head in their direction and eyed them suspiciously for several seconds.

It must have felt like hours to the horrified men. Finally, she cleared her throat of muck and began to speak. Her foul smelling breath made them gag, which brought her great amusement. The years had not dulled her sharp tongue.

"So…YOU are the valiant ones who have brought me back from the depths of the bog. Are you not pleased with your results? Do not quiver like frightened children. Vixiana will not harm you."

Murphy straightened up and addressed her, grasping the amulet in front of him with both hands all the while like a warrior's shield. "Witch of the tor, I am the one who has brought you back from the dead. You are bound to my will. Do not harm us."

Vixiana let out a high pitched laugh that forced them to cower momentarily. "Yes, yes, that is true. But many in the past had wished for my death. Why is it that YOU desired to grant me life once more?"

Murphy mustered up some fake courage. "That is not your concern, witch. For the present, I demand that you stay hidden in your cave and not climb up on your tor or venture out onto the moor. It is vital to our plans that your existence remains a secret. Do you understand?"

The hag scowled, and then muttered something unintelligible. By all appearance, her form and features had remained the same, except that her skin had become severely tanned and leathery from the years submerged in the bog. The acids in the peat had preserved her body much like the way fruit is sustained by pickling, while the cool temperatures and lack of oxygen prevented decomposition.

She replied to his question with resignation. "I am bound by the powers of darkness to obey, and cannot do otherwise. But I desire food after all these years, AND a moment's pleasure. Can you grant me a boon?"

She eyed Murphy expectantly, and he did not disappoint. "I was told to expect such requests. Hold here a moment."

He walked back around the tor, leaving Stapleton alone to face Vixiana. Jack felt vulnerable without Murphy and his amulet, so he was relieved when his partner returned shortly pulling a small goat behind him. Murphy handed the rope to Vixiana.

"This should satisfy BOTH your requests. Now we must go. Remember my orders, AND your allegiance to me, old hag."

Murphy motioned to Stapleton that it was high time to leave. As they made their way back to the tin mine in the Grimpen Mire, Jack's curiosity got the better of him. He had to ask the question that was on his mind.

"What exactly did you mean when you said satisfy BOTH your requests? I understand that the goat will provide her with meat, but what about the moment's pleasure?"

Murphy shot him a look of disbelief. "Fool! She will keep the goat tethered, toss it into the bog, then watch and listen as it struggles in vain until sucked under the muck. Once dead, she will pull it back out and...feast. It will keep her under control for a brief period.

Jack was impressed. "You are thinking ahead Murphy. I like that. With any luck, by the time she craves more, we will have discovered the chink in Sir Henry's armor to use against him. But always remember, you control the witch, but I am the key to your fortune."

His tone of voice then changed to one of resentment. "The fork in the road is just ahead. Go back to your warm bed in the village; I will return to the filthy mine that is my home. But that will soon change. Sir Henry, I hope you are sleeping peacefully tonight."

In fact, the baronet had a wonderful night's sleep, so much so that he was in high spirits the following day at breakfast. He was quick to greet Homes and Watson as they entered the dining area.

"Well, gentlemen. I trust that you are satisfied with your rooms. I am told by Mrs. Barrymore that our beds here at the hall are quite comfortable, but then again, I suspect that anything would be an improvement over the accommodations from your previous stay on Dartmoor, wouldn't you think, Mr.

Holmes?"

He was forced to agree. "Without a doubt, Sir Henry. Living among the stone huts was a necessary deception on my part, but one that I would prefer NOT to duplicate, at least not so soon. I don't believe that my back has yet to fully recover. By the by, how are your ribs feeling this morning?"

"Excellent, Mr. Holmes. I must say, Watson, that you did a first rate job last night readjusting my bandages. I am able to breathe normally, yet there is still firm support for my flank. I am obliged to you."

The doctor beamed. Although he and Holmes were good friends, it was not in the detective's nature to be free flowing with compliments. This was also quite possibly the only praise he would receive for the day, so he basked in its fleeting delight. Holmes noted it and smiled ever so slightly.

The squire continued. "So my friends, I should tell you up front that Laura's...rather Mrs. Lyons ...divorce has been completed. I plan on breaking the news to her during a picnic out on the moor this afternoon. I hope you have no objections to my making these arrangements without your knowledge."

Watson balked. "Do you think that is a wise idea, Sir Henry? After all, obviously we cannot come with you, and we have yet to discover who is still trying to harm you."

Holmes responded. "I do not believe that Sir Henry will be in any imminent danger so long as he does not venture out ALONE on the moor. I stated that the last time I was here on Dartmoor, Sir Henry, and I repeat it now. You must not go out alone, particularly at NIGHT. Do I have your assurance on this stipulation?"

The squire's face suddenly turned serious, and he nodded in agreement. "As you wish, Mr. Holmes. And what, if I may ask, do you gentlemen plan on doing today? How will you begin your investigations once more into my case?"

The doctor gushed out a reply. "We have already begun. Why, only last night Holmes theorized that..."

The detective broke in. "I theorized that Dr. Watson would be unable to resist revealing any information that we may have acquired." There was an awkward pause.

"I think we shall start first in the village and make some inquiries. Perhaps there is some vital clue that had escaped us on our last go round. That should fully occupy our time until supper I imagine. Perhaps we could presume to make use of the carriage by having Perkins drop us off at the Grimpen Post Office, Sir Henry?"

The baronet cheerfully agreed. "Of course, Mr. Holmes. I shall see to it at once. However, I will be taking the trap by myself early in the afternoon over to Coombe Tracey to pick up Laura for our picnic on the moor. I do not know the exact time that I shall be taking her home. I trust you do not mind making other travel arrangements for your return?"

Watson replied for his friend. "It is a beautiful day, Sir Henry. We will have no objection to walking if necessary. Just make certain that YOU are back here within the safety of these walls before nightfall."

CHAPTER 11

A Chance Encounter

Laura Lyons stood in front of her lodging house in Coombe Tracey and waited patiently for the carriage to arrive. She was outfitted in a striking teal colored dress and emerald green shawl, with a white bonnet to keep the sun from her eyes. A wicker woven picnic basket dangled at her side. There was no doubt among the locals as to how she was going to pass this beautiful fall day. The only question was with whom, although they had their suspicions.

They did not have long to wait for their answer. The Baskerville carriage lumbered up the main road into the village and gradually stopped beside her. Sir Henry climbed down from the driver's seat and greeted her with a smile, which was instantly returned.

"My word, Laura; that is a fetching outfit you have on, if I may say so. You look lovely."

The words were pure poetry to a woman who had seen so many personal hardships, and they did not go unappreciated. "Why thank you Henry. I must admit that it does my heart good to hear you say so. But I did find it strange to see you driving the coach and not Perkins. If you would help me into the carriage we can…"

Henry interrupted. "I thought you might ride up top alongside me. It is a lovely day, and I can attest that the breeze is wonderful. Do you mind?"

Laura was briefly surprised but recovered quickly. "Of...of course. I would like that very much. You may help me UP then."

In a few moments they were riding out of the village. As the coach sped by St. George's Church, they caught sight of Reverend Musgrave, who waved to them eagerly and tipped his hat. He appeared to Laura to be very pleased.

"My, the reverend seems in good spirits today, Henry. Why do you think?"

He pretended to think for a moment. "Cleanliness is close to godliness, or perhaps the vicar's happy the church roof repairs are completed."

She looked at him with uncertainty but let it go. Then, just as they were leaving the outskirts of the village, Laura began to giggle. Now Henry returned the look.

"I give up. What's so funny?"

"Us! Did you notice the strange looks on the faces of all the people we passed? I imagine it is not often that a baronet and his escort are seen riding on the OUTSIDE of their carriage."

Henry smiled. "Yes, I believe that would be a peculiar sight for the local citizenry, now that you mention it. I hope that I'm driving in the right direction. Do you have a particular spot in mind for our picnic? I confess that I am still new to the moor."

"I do, and it's not far from here. Go on another few miles. We'll stop by Doyle's Tor. There is a wonderful place nearby. I would often go there when I...needed to think."

In a few minutes time they found themselves facing a wide, squat tor situated just off the main road. They ventured past it on foot and in less than a quarter of a mile, the couple was in the midst of a rolling green section of the moor where few bothered to venture. It was a beautiful and secluded spot that matched the flawless fall day. Laura went to great pains to spread out the blanket and display the picnic provisions in just the right arrangement. After all, this was their first meal alone together.

They had a leisurely lunch of French bread, cold meats and cheese, with fruit tarts that Laura had made herself for dessert. Most of all, they thoroughly enjoyed each other's company, with conversation flowing as easily as though they had known each other for years. Finally, there was a short pause, and Sir Henry made use of it while they sat comfortably on a blanket.

"Laura, I spoke with my solicitor's while in London to meet with Mr. Holmes and Dr. Watson. I am happy to tell you that your divorce papers have been finalized. Your former husband will no longer trouble you in any way. He has accepted the terms offered to him, and you are once again a free woman…to do whatever you wish, and go wherever you want."

She stared at him in near disbelief, as though just then realizing the abrupt change it would bring to her life. "So he is gone then…gone forever, like waking from a bad dream. How I prayed for this day to arrive. I almost thought that it never would, but YOU changed all that, Henry, in more ways than you can imagine."

He reached over and took her hand. "I think I can, but I want to hear it from YOU, Laura. I love you, and wish that you would allow me the opportunity to make you happy. Will you do so?"

She smiled and returned his gaze. "Yes, Henry, I will do so. But…what will people say? Perhaps…"

He broke in. "I have already spoken to Reverend Musgrave. He is aware of the divorce and has given me, or I should say US, his blessing. Word will get out that there is nothing unseemly between us; that is another reason why I wanted you to ride outside on top of the carriage with me, so that all could see."

"Oh Henry, I DO love you, and I will strive to make our life together a happy one."

They kissed softly, and as they did so, there came a rustling sound from behind a nearby rock outcropping. The proceedings were being watched the entire time. The couple looked quickly in the direction of the noise, and that was when they saw it. Laura gasped and drew back, while the startled baronet, unable to break his stare, reached blindly on the blanket for a knife.

For a few moments, nothing happened; then, with a slow and steady limp, the largest dog either of them had ever seen in their lives ventured forward and dropped down on its stomach right in front of them.

It had a huge square shaped skull, with massive forelegs set wide apart. The beast must have been three feet tall and was shaped like a stout wooden keg. It had a black muzzle, but the color extended up and over to include its eyes and ears, giving off the impression of a sinister dark mask. The rest of the body possessed a smooth coat of brindle. Its flews were pink, along with a substantial dew lap that drooped lazily from its cheeks. The pupils of its eyes were jet black, while the irises were a soft brown.

It breathed heavily and gazed back and forth between Sir Henry and the food spread out on the blanket, as though deciding what next course of action to undertake. Drool began to fall from its muzzle as it continued to eye the provisions. Although quite large, the dog's ribs were beginning to show. Dried blood had matted and stained its right front paw, which had been cut. This injury had obviously seriously curtailed its ability to fend for itself.

Sir Henry was the first to break the silence. "Why, I believe I have seen this dog once before, while we were on our way back to Coombe Tracey. It was following the carriage off on the side of the road. Perkins said it was probably a wild moor dog that smelled the lunch his wife had prepared. It appears to have done the same once again."

Laura was still puzzled. "But this is no normal sized dog, Henry, and it is not one of the usual sheep dogs that strike out on their own to desert cruel masters. This is a mastiff, unusual for the moor, and I wouldn't be surprised if it was well over two hundred pounds, for heaven's sake. Shall I...give it some food?"

Henry chuckled. "Well, I don't suppose it stopped by to admire your bonnet. But we don't know this dog's temperament. Better let me try. Let's stay seated on the blanket so it doesn't think we are making any hostile moves."

He picked out a wedge of chicken and gradually leaned forward, placing it just in front of the dog's snout. While the squire did so, the dog focused its attention not on the meat but on Sir Henry's exposed throat, yet did nothing. Finally, it sniffed the chicken with increasing interest, then slowly opened its mouth and gently took the food into its jaws and swallowed it whole.

Laura was pleased. "Well, that's a promising start to your new friendship. Why don't I load up a plate and you can slide it in front of him. I'm sure this poor beast is famished."

As Henry nodded his approval, she heaped on one delicacy after another to the point where the china could no longer be seen. He picked it up with both hands and began to place it in front of the mastiff, but as he did so, he noticed that the dog was sniffing his hands and staring intently at him, as though familiar with the scent. It made the squire stop for a moment, and their eyes met. It was a strange portrait, one that had Laura holding her breath in fearful anticipation. She knew that although injured and weak, this beast could finish them both off with very little effort.

Finally, Henry took the chance and dropped the plate at the foot of the dog's enormous front paws. The animal broke its gaze and plunged its face into the mountain of life sustaining food with a vengeance. The couple sat and watched in quiet satisfaction until nothing remained.

Laura spoke up. "I've had a few dogs in my youth, Henry. The thing they love best after a good meal is a drink of water. I brought some for cleaning the dishes before repacking them. Empty the fruit from that bowl. I'll pour it in and you can give it to him."

The baronet followed her direction, and presently a clear, clean bowl of water was being lapped up gratefully by the beast with great relish. Hunting sufficient food on the moor was one thing, but finding fresh water was nearly unheard of. It must have tasted like liquid gold to an animal used to the foul smelling, brackish pools found on the heaths, and ultimately, this simple element was the one item that changed the equation.

The dog emptied the bowl and then looked up at the squire with a cocked head and puzzled expression, as though unable to comprehend what had just happened. Finally, it moved slowly over to him and lay down, putting its head on top of his crossed leg. Laura registered genuine shock.

"Why, Henry, I believe this wild one has decided to reward you with its friendship. Look, he's actually closing his eyes and…going to SLEEP! This is a great honor, whether you realize it or not. I'll quietly start putting things back into the carriage. You stay with your new companion for a while longer."

The dog kept its eyes closed, but its ears twitched ever so slightly with each sound or tonal inflection. Henry took his hand and gently began to stroke the dog's head. He wondered how long it had been since a human hand had done so, if at all.

Laura finished her packing and returned to them. "Well, all that's left is you and the blanket you're sitting on. I have an idea. Why don't you try his ear?"

"TRY HIS EAR? What do you mean?"

Laura laughed. "I can see that you don't know much about dogs, do you Henry? If you really want to make a dog be completely at ease, you slowly put your finger into its ear and gradually move it around. Trust me."

The squire was skeptical, but Laura's sincerity convinced him to give it at least one try. Not quite knowing if this would lead to a limb being ripped off, he inched his hand to the side of the dog's head and delicately lifted its ear flap. He waited, and when nothing happened, he did as Laura suggested with his forefinger. This instantly led to the dog leaning its head towards him and emitting a low moan of pleasure. A lengthy exhale of air followed shortly thereafter, a sign that it was completely at ease.

"Why, Laura, you're absolutely correct. We have certainly performed a good Christian act by saving this poor beast from starvation. The cut in the dog's paw looks scabbed over, so I trust it won't be long before he can resume his steady hunt for food. Let us be off then."

But that was easier said than done. As the couple made their way to the carriage, the animal roused itself and followed close behind in Sir Henry's footsteps. For a moment they thought it had finally decided to attack them, but when they climbed up without incident into the driver's seat, the dog gave out a quick bark and stared at the baronet. To Laura, the explanation was obvious.

"Henry, I do believe that this beast has chosen you... AS ITS MASTER! Why don't we take it back with us?"

He was astonished. "Do you REALLY think so? I suppose there's just one way to find out. How do YOU feel about it, my four legged friend? If I opened the carriage door like this would you climb right up and lie down quietly while we return to Baskerville Hall?"

Although there did appear to be a few seconds of hesitation, the dog ambled up to the coach and jumped up and into the cab with a flourish, then made three tight knit circles and lay down on the floor. The baronet closed the door gently and looked back at Laura.

"Well, my dear, it appears that I have THREE guardians at the moment. I wonder what Mr. Holmes and Dr. Watson would say about this new development. Now that I think of it, I believe that they should be just about finished with a portion of their follow up investigation in Grimpen."

And how right he was, although it was proving to be less than enlightening. The two were just concluding their inquiry at the final stop, the village post office and police station. Holmes was pacing in a corner of Sergeant Bullfinches back office while the doctor sat on a three legged stool nearby watching him grow more and more agitated.

"So, sergeant, you are totally convinced that the servant Antonio HAS left the area. This is extremely important."

Bullfinch was adamant. "Of that I'm certain, Mr. Holmes. Once you uncovered the plot against Sir Henry and foiled Mr. Stapleton's plan, he has not been seen anywhere on or around Dartmoor. I made further inquiries with the police in Townsend, Kelly Bray, Gunnislake, and even went as far away as Yelverton and Tavistock; no stranger matching his description has been sighted. I continue to believe that he has fled the country altogether."

Holmes wore his disappointment on his sleeve. He stopped pacing and his shoulders dropped. "Thank you, sergeant. It's just that I am fully convinced that there is another agent in this region bent on Sir Henry's destruction. Have there been any newcomers to Grimpen since we were last here?"

"No, Mr. Holmes. There has been an occasional traveler, but no one has stayed for more than a few days. Perhaps the incidents swirling around Sir Henry are just bad luck. After all, the Baskerville family has seen more than its share of misfortune over the years, and it is well documented."

Watson answered. "I was also of that belief, sergeant, but if Mr. Holmes feels that something is amiss, then you can depend upon it. Although we have also spoken to Reverend Musgrave and Mayor Sexton without success, I too feel that there is a dark cloud hovering over Sir Henry. I daresay it is all of our best interests that we get to the bottom of this."

Bullfinch nodded. "That is true, doctor. The squire's generosity is already on display. The new church roof is magnificent, and soon the workmen will arrive from London to repair the roads and bridges."

Holmes perked up. "Is that so? This could work to our advantage, gentlemen. With crews out and about the countryside on a daily basis, the movements of our adversary will be somewhat restricted should he...or she... wish to remain hidden. We must speak to Sir Henry when we return to the hall.

Well, that about wraps things up here in the village. Thank you for your help, sergeant. I must admit that I relish the thought of basking in front of a roaring fire after one of Mrs. Barrymore's fine meals. Come Watson; let us procure transportation back to the manor."

Unbeknownst to the great detective, that spot had already been taken. When Holmes and Watson finally entered the great hall, they beheld a serene but strange sight. Sir Henry was seated comfortably in his usual high backed chair, but lying beside him with its back to the fire was the huge dog from the moor.

It was relaxing, yet on guard at the same time, as the animal was facing outward to obtain a view of anyone coming into the room. When it noticed the two men enter, it stood up and watched them intensely as they cautiously approached the squire. Sir Henry rose to his feet and patted the top of the dog's head to offer it reassurance. He could not help but greet them with an awkward grin.

"Ahh, gentlemen, I see that you have returned. Did you uncover any valuable information whilst in town?"

Watson replied, but his eyes were fixed on the dog. "We came up empty, I'm afraid, at least for the moment. But I see that YOU did not return empty handed from your picnic. Is that a moor pony you have there, Sir Henry? It's certainly big enough."

The baronet laughed heartily. "No doctor, it IS a dog, I assure you; a mastiff to be exact…according to Laura. I know little of dogs, except for the one in the family legend. It was injured and must have been starving.

Once the smell of the food wafted out onto the moor, it hobbled into our quiet gathering, and after a good meal, seemed to become rather attached to me. As a matter of fact, he has not left my side since I entered the hall. I must say it is oddly reassuring to have such a bodyguard as this following me about. What do you make of it Mr. Holmes? Do you approve?"

Holmes studied the dog carefully before crafting his reply. "Absolutely, Sir Henry. I must say it is not uncommon for a dog to form a bond with someone who has done it a good turn in time of need, but…I am puzzled about its breeding. I would have expected a wild SHEEP dog from the moor rather than this gigantic beast. Have you given it a name, by chance?"

The baronet was silent for a moment, and then looked at the new friend by his side. "Now that you mention it, I have not. Well, if you're going to be staying with us, my friend, you must have a name. What do you say to…Shadow? You DO follow me everywhere."

The dog displayed no outward show of emotion, but appeared to enjoy the sound of Sir Henry's voice, no matter what he was saying. The squire scratched under the dog's chin.

"Well then, Shadow it is from here on in. Gentlemen, you must be hungry. I have already instructed Mrs. Barrymore to prepare supper for your arrival. I shall ring for Barrymore to bring it into the dining room."

Holmes broke in. "By the way, Sir Henry, Sergeant Bullfinch mentioned that the workmen your general contractor hired for the road and bridge repairs will arrive shortly. Is that correct?"

"Yes, Mr. Holmes. They will arrive by the end of next week, along with all of the materials needed. They will be put up in Grimpen and Coombe Tracey . Why do you ask?"

"They may be of assistance in our daily observations. I still believe that there is someone here whom we have overlooked. It must be a person familiar to all; therefore he she would be above suspicion, even to the police."

"I am sure you are right, Mr. Holmes, and take no offense, but now that I have such a constant bodyguard at my side, I am finally beginning to feel safe at long last. By the way, I have invited some friends to dinner tomorrow night. I trust that your investigations will allow you to attend?"

"By all means, Sir Henry. We will look forward to it. I daresay this will keep the Barrymores quite busy, wouldn't you say Watson?"

The doctor was caught off guard by the question, but understood why it was asked. "I suspect that they will have certainly their hands full for the dinner party. Perhaps that's a good thing. Idle hands are the devil's workshop, ay Holmes?"

Now Sir Henry was caught off guard. "Yes, I suppose you are correct, but I hope this doesn't mean that you now..."

Holmes cut in. "We are reviewing all previous players in this ongoing Shakespearean tragedy of sorts, Sir Henry. There is no need to be surprised. Will Dr. Mortimer be on the guest list by chance?"

"Yes, Mr. Holmes. I thought it would do him good to get out of the house for a bit. I am sure that it is lonely for him there now in the evening hours."

"Excellent; tomorrow's gathering will also give me an opportunity to speak to the good doctor in an informal setting. There are some items I need to clear up about his wife's recent death."

As the three men continued with their conversation, only Shadow noticed that the door leading to the dining room moved ever so slightly. Barrymore was on the other side listening, with his wife not far behind him. His face became red with anger as he turned to Eliza.

"Mr. Holmes considers us suspects ONCE AGAIN!"

CHAPTER 12

Death On The Moor

A solitary figure stood outside of Baskerville Hall, putting the silver, hound faced knocker to good use on the massive wooden doors. The response was swift as Barrymore, dressed in his butler's best, swung the door open with a smile and stood sharply at attention.

"Good evening, Dr. Mortimer! It is so good to see you again. Sir Henry and the others are in the front parlor. Will you be so kind as to follow me?"

The doctor scoffed. "Dash it all, Barrymore, I should hope to know my way around the hall by now. I'm sure that you and your wife will be very busy tonight. You go and help her; I'll find my way to the parlor...and thank you for coming to my wife's service. It was greatly appreciated."

Barrymore quickly disappeared from sight as Mortimer took a deep breath and made his way to the parlor. It was his first social engagement since his wife's death, and he felt uncomfortable without her. The smell of pipe tobacco grew stronger as he approached the room, and he was able to identify the voices engaged in conversation. After a moment's hesitation, he walked in and looked about. He did not get an opportunity to speak, as Sir Henry spied him immediately.

"James! How good of you to come. I was afraid that you might have changed your mind at the last moment. Come in and make yourself comfortable. You know everyone here, so there is no need for Victorian formalities, which I attempt to circumvent as much as possible. Can I interest you in some sherry before dinner?"

"Why yes, that would be nice. Reverend, Mayor Sexton, Mr. Frankland, Mr. Holmes, Dr. Watson…good evening. I hope that I have not interrupted your discussion?"

Musgrave replied quickly. "No, not at all, James. Actually, we were just discussing the newest member of the Baskerville family. Have you met him yet?"

Mortimer stood in surprised silence. The squire rescued his friend and answered for him. "No, Reverend, I do not believe that James has had the pleasure. Shadow…come here, my good boy."

With that, the mastiff rose from a darkened corner of the room, trotted up to his master, and leaned faintly against his leg in a sign of affection. However, due to the dog's size and weight, the baronet lost his balance and shuffled his feet to remain erect. He laughed and rubbed under the dog's chin.

Mortimer was dumbfounded. "Good God! Is it real? Where did you find that…thing, Henry, and more importantly, is it safe?"

Mayor Sexton cleared his throat and gave a pensive response. "We were discussing that very subject when you arrived, James. The squire found the dog starving while out on the moor and brought it back with him. Food has overcome its fear, but more importantly, since the baronet supplied the tasty fare, the animal has decided to become a member of Sir Henry's pack, so to speak; at least that is what we can surmise to this point."

Dr. Watson spoke up. "Gentlemen, I find this to be an absolutely incredible set of circumstances. I am sure that the irony of this situation is not lost on any of you. Sir Henry's malevolent relative, Hugo Baskerville, was ripped to pieces by a wild hound, and now the present lord of the manor is under the protection of another. You have been unusually quiet about all of this, Holmes. What do you make of it?"

All eyes focused on the great detective. Before he spoke, he turned to Musgrave. "Pardon me, Reverend, but are you familiar with the Hindu or Buddhist concept of…karma?"

The vicar gave out an uneasy chuckle. "Why, no Mr. Holmes, I am afraid that eastern religions are a bit out of my line, so to speak. What does this have to do with Sir Henry?"

Holmes smiled. "Perhaps everything, IF one has an open mind. You see, the Sanskrit word karma means action or deed, and the intent of that action has a direct influence on the future of a certain individual. Taking it one step further, good intent and good deeds will result in future happiness, while bad intent and foul deeds results in future misery. Can you see where I'm going with this, Sir Henry?"

The baronet was listening intently and was quick to answer. "I…I believe I do, Mr. Homes. This all relates to my family history, doesn't it? My infamous ancestor, Sir Hugo, was a cruel and evil man, and he would eventually be torn apart by the Hound of Hell."

Holmes was pleased. "Quite right, Sir Henry; while you, on the other hand, have given graciously to civic and spiritual improvements that benefit your community's citizenry and the surrounding region. Also, by feeding this dog instead of taking a confrontational stance and driving it off in its hour of need, it would appear that you now have a loyal friend for life."

Musgrave interrupted; his voice contained a slight tone of irritation. "So, Mr. Holmes, you hold with Buddhism rather than Christianity?"

Holmes was taken back for a moment. "By no means, Reverend. I am an OBSERVER, first and foremost, as Dr. Watson would be the first to attest. I am interested in many things, particularly various religious beliefs. While the major faiths of the world clash with one another for supremacy, I take the view that whatever creed makes someone a better PERSON should be the focus of our concern. The world would certainly be a better place if we prescribed to that notion."

Sir Henry observed the vicar carefully and sensed that he was about to issue a stinging rebuttal. Fortunately, Barrymore entered and gave him the signal that supper was ready, and he seized upon the moment.

"Gentlemen, let us retire to the dining hall. Barrymore, what delicacies has your good wife prepared for us tonight?"

"If I may be so bold sir, her special almond soup to begin, followed by roast turkey with potatoes and asparagus tips. I believe the desserts are napoleon cakes and compote of cherries."

Dr. Watson's pace quickened at the sound of it all, which drew some veiled amusement from the remaining guests. Holmes was the last person to leave the room, followed shortly thereafter by Shadow, who kept a watchful eye on his master at the head of the entourage. Holmes felt a slight chill knowing that such an animal was close behind him, but he refused to look back. After all, what was there to fear?

Sir Henry soon motioned everyone into the dining hall. "Please be seated wherever you wish, gentlemen. There are no name cards signifying place settings at THIS table. I so dislike that custom."

Watson jockeyed for position and sat between the vicar and Holmes on one side of the table. The baronet gave a slight sigh of relief and nodded to the good doctor, who felt Sir Henry's silent appreciation. Mortimer and the mayor sat on the other side, while the mastiff walked to corner of the room and lay down facing his master.

Sexton was impressed. "My word, this dog certainly knows enough not to beg for food, Sir Henry. How on earth did you accomplish that? Did you not say that it was living wild on the moor?"

The squire laughed. "There is no trick to it at all. I simply fed him exceedingly well before you all arrived, and I must say, Shadow wolfed down an impressive amount of food. He is quite content now, I assure you. Of course, he did not receive any dessert, so I may slip him a napoleon cake before I retire. It appears that I am spoiling him already, I'm afraid."

The mayor changed the focus as the soup was brought out by the Barrymores. "Mr. Holmes, I understand from Sir Henry that you are back in Dartmoor to tidy up some loose ends from your previous stay so that Dr. Watson can complete a story for The Strand Magazine. Is that correct?"

The detective's expression did not change, and neither did the baronet's, but Watson's face turned a particularly light shade of pink. Only Mortimer and Laura knew the true purpose of the return visit, as it would arose less suspicion, although Sergeant Bullfinch must have had a strong suspicion.

Holmes felt the need to reply. "Yes, Dr. Watson has become quite the author, at least to those who purchase that particular publication. I thought that I would indulge him while taking Sir Henry up on his previous invitation to return for a visit."

The vicar was nearly finished his soup when he decided to continue sparring with Holmes. He was still irritated by the conversation in the parlor. "So, Mr. Holmes, do you believe in God?"

The detective could sense that the vicar was spoiling for a fight. Nothing could be worse than discussing religion and politics at a dinner table, so he did his best to diffuse the situation for his host's sake.

"Why...yes, reverend, I most certainly do."

Musgrave was assuaged, but now the mayor's interest was piqued. "Can we then assume that you also believe in the supernatural?"

Now here was a subject that held great interest for Holmes, and frankly, for everyone present at the table. Spiritualism was all the rage of Victorian England, with many people fervently swearing allegiance to the great beyond.

"I neither believe nor disbelieve in the supernatural, Mr. Sexton. I would like to express some measure of confidence in its existence, but I have yet to see proof, that is, actual scientific proof."

The mayor was surprised. "Mr. Holmes, when you first heard the story of the Hound of the Baskervilles from Dr. Mortimer, can you actually say that you did not believe that you were stepping into a realm beyond the natural world?"

Watson flew to the defense of his friend. "I will have you know, Mr. Sexton, that Holmes believed we were dealing with a flesh and blood antagonist as early as our meeting with Sir Henry in London, when he reported missing one of his boots at the hotel."

Holmes beamed. "Good old Watson. Yes, as early as that, I am afraid, Mr. Sexton. I gathered that the devil's agents were flesh and blood, and therefore using the hound story as a smokescreen to perpetrate a horrible crime of murder for profit."

Mortimer interjected in an almost pleading voice. "Have you then not encountered ANY elements of the supernatural in your many cases, Mr. Holmes?"

The detective shook his head with great regret. "The closest I had come to encountering the supernatural was a few years back. I believe Dr. Watson called the case The Adventure of the Sussex Vampire. It was a very interesting situation, make no mistake. A man called upon me in distress, believing that his Peruvian wife was sucking the blood out of their infant son.

Well, to make a long story short, I discovered that their jealous older half-brother was shooting poisoned darts at the child, and the mother was actually sucking out the poison in an effort to save the baby's life. So you can see that it's in the interpretation of facts where we miss the mark and go astray, gentlemen."

The room grew quiet and the mood somber after Holmes' soliloquy, but the moment was saved when the Barrymores brought in the main course. It was polished off in short order, with many kudos offered up to Eliza, who accepted them graciously while she and her husband removed the plates from the table. Holmes smiled as he watched Watson rustle impatiently in his chair.

The thought of the impending napoleon cakes and cherry compote was first and foremost on the doctor's mind, and he was delighted with his decision to save some appetite for dessert, for they were simply superb. All that was left to top off a fine evening was brandy and cigars, but Sir Henry had an important matter to discuss and he could no longer contain himself.

"Mr. Frankland, might I have a word with you privately in the drawing room while the others relax? It will not take long I assure you."

Frankland was taken off guard for a moment. "I hope this is not about my latest litigation, Sir Henry. I don't know if anyone has asked you to speak on their behalf, but I received the judgment in my favor and I plan to make sure that..."

The squire waved him off. "No, no, it's nothing like that. Please, if you would give me but a moment of your time."

The two left the dining hall together and ventured into the drawing room, where Sir Henry quickly closed the door behind him. Frankland decided not to get comfortable, and stood in the middle of the room with his hands hanging onto the lapels of his suit jacket as though bracing for bad news of some sort. He was not to be disappointed.

Sir Henry cleared his throat before speaking. "Mr. Frankland, I believe that you should hear this from my own lips, as it does affect you sir. As you may know, your daughter Laura has endeavored for some time to obtain a divorce from her present husband. I…"

Frankland exploded. "She would not be in this position if she did not marry against my expressed wishes. The man was the worst sort of fellow, but she was blind to it. Now she has the temerity to live apart from her own husband. She has brought disgrace to me and upon our family name. In addition, I recently found out that Sir Charles was assisting her financially behind my back."

The baronet grew tense. "What my late uncle did was an act of Christian charity. And if you thought that HE deceived you, then I suspect that you will feel all the more betrayed by what I am about to tell you."

Frankland cocked his head and spoke slowly. "Just what do you mean by that statement?"

"What I mean is that my solicitors in London have obtained a legal and binding divorce for her, which means that Laura is now a free woman. What's more, she and I have fallen in love. I would hope that for all our sakes you would forgive your daughter's past indiscretion and…"

Frankland grew red in the face. "Marriage is not an indiscretion, but rather a sacred institution that she has cast aside like yesterday's newspaper. But it is not as simple as that sir. You Baskervilles think that you can meddle into the lives of those about you as though this was some type of game; well, it is not."

Sir Henry was puzzled. "But don't you understand what I am trying to tell you? Your daughter, your own flesh, will finally be happy and secure in this world. How can you not feel anything but joy that her life will be..."

"She DISGRACED me, sir! I will have nothing further to do with her or you. BARRYMORE, GET ME MY HAT AND COAT AT ONCE!"

The tone of the old man's voice produced an immediate response from poor Barrymore, and Frankland was shortly stomping towards the front door. The rest of the company surmised what had just happened, as they were well aware of the budding romance. In truth, they welcomed it.

Nevertheless, they sat quiet and still as church mice, unwilling to get caught in the crossfire of this extremely sticky situation. Only Shadow appeared willing to enter the fray. He stood up with his ears twitching at the sounds of discord, waiting for a call from his master.

Sir Henry made one last attempt to quench the fire. "Mr. Frankland, it is several miles back to Lafter Hall. Please wait a moment and let me have Perkins drive you home."

Frankland wagged his finger in the squire's face. "I want nothing from you, sir, and in the future, I want nothing to do with you OR that divorced woman. She is dead to me, and that is the last word that I will ever have on this subject."

He abruptly turned and walked out the door and into the dark night. There was no moon to speak of, so the trek back would be difficult, even for a local. Sir Henry watched him depart with mixed feelings, and then returned to the dining hall to fulfill his duties as host. All could see that the confrontation with Frankland had drained him.

"I must offer you my apologies, gentlemen. Obviously, things did not go as I had hoped."

Reverend Musgrave attempted to prop up the dejected squire's spirits. "There was nothing you could have done to assuage him, Sir Henry. I have known Mr. Frankland for many years. He is a proud, stubborn man, with rigid beliefs that do not allow compromise. Accept his decision and move on without him."

Mortimer was in agreement. "The vicar has spoken wisely, Henry. You have friends here and in the village who will be supportive to both you and Laura. Perhaps, in time, even someone as obstinate as Frankland will soften and see the light of reason. I just wish that some of that light would follow him tonight. It is nearly pitch black outside. A man can hardly see his hand in front of his face."

Unfortunately, the doctor's statement was all too true. Initially, Frankland felt considerable pent up rage directed towards Sir Henry and his daughter, and it worked in his favor. He was able to walk at a brisk pace over the moor towards Lafter Hall without much of a sustained effort, and when he lost sight of the road ahead, he would glance down occasionally and barely make out the side of the road. This at least kept him going in the right direction.

However, as he neared Vixen Tor, a thick mist suddenly blew across the road. Frankland stopped momentarily in his tracks, and he became completely disoriented. After a moment, he took a few faltering steps, but his foot hit a stone embedded in the top of the roadbed and he fell forward and struck the ground like a falling tree. There was not even enough time for him to push his hands out in front to cushion the fall.

Frankland hit face first and broke his nose, although initially he did not know it. He gave out a quick cry of pain, but only when he began bleeding profusely down into his mouth did he realize the severity of the accident. He wiped the blood away with a swipe of his sleeve and slowly rose to his knees. With a deep breath he stood up and looked around. It was as though he were a bird flying into a cloud; he could see absolutely nothing but whitish gray fog.

Frankland had full knowledge of fog banks creeping up on moor folk, having lived on Dartmoor for many years, but this one seemed to come upon him from out of nowhere. He knew his best course of action was to wait it out and not go traipsing about the countryside, so he inched his way along the road until he felt a boulder just off the side of the road. There he perched himself and waited for the breeze to blow the fog by him, but it did no such thing. The temperature began to drop, and he found himself starting to shiver. Just as he began to resign himself to a terrible night, he heard a female voice cut through the fog.

"HELLOOOOO! Is somebody there? I thought I heard a cry a few moments ago."

Frankland was ecstatic. "YES! YES! I am over in this direction good woman. I am lost in this blasted fog. Do you live nearby?"

The voice answered. "I do indeed, but I am old and cannot move about well. Follow my voice and I will lead you to safety."

Frankland did as he was instructed and followed the voice. He never realized that he had ambled off the main road and onto the heath, as he was so preoccupied in listening for his savior's directions. Suddenly, he took a step and his right foot sunk into a mucky substance and he began to lose his balance once again. In an effort to stay upright, he thrust his left foot out in front, and that too sunk, this time up to his knee.

He tried to move either foot, but they were stuck, and now sinking deeper. It was then he realized that he had stepped into a bog. A wave of fear swept over him as he screamed for the woman in a tone of desperation.

"PLEASE, I HAVE WALKED INTO A BOG! COME THIS WAY AND SAVE ME BEFORE IT IS TOO LATE!

No sooner had he spoken those words than the fog dissipated and he spied an old woman standing nearby. It was Vixiana. She was smiling from ear to ear and rubbing her hands together in delight. Frankland felt a cold chill settle over him as their eyes met, but he did not understand its meaning as of yet. He was more concerned with his continuous sinking into the bog. He was now in up to his hips.

He was incredulous. "What are you waiting for? I am close to the edge. Just give me your hand for a moment and I can pull myself out!"

Vixiana began to laugh uncontrollably in pure joy. It had been centuries since she had dispatched anyone in this fashion, and she was savoring every second of it. Frankland was now in up to his chest, and he began to hyperventilate as he realized that help was not forthcoming.

He thrashed about in an unsuccessful attempt to extricate himself, but that only made it worse. He found himself in up to his neck.

Frankland made one final plea before going under. "For the love of God, please help me! I will give you anything you desire!"

Vixiana responded thoughtfully. "What I desire more than anything...is your DEATH!"

CHAPTER 13

Muddy Waters

Watson sat contently in the dining hall. He had just consumed a splendid breakfast. Holmes had watched him throughout the repast with a mixture of admiration and bemusement.

"Watson, do you think of anything besides your stomach when you wake in the morning?"

The good doctor paused to reflect for a moment. "Well…now that you mention it, Holmes, I can't come up with anything of a pressing nature. But why must you look down upon my culinary gratifications? It's not MY fault that you eat like a bird."

Sir Henry laughed heartily at the two good comrades. "Gentlemen, you remind me of an old married couple who continually get on each other's nerves but could not conceivably do without one another. What do you make of all this, Shadow?"

The mastiff was lying by the fireplace but picked its head up when he heard his master's voice. Holmes was impressed.

"Sir Henry, you have only had that dog but a few days, and yet it already is cognizant of the name you have bestowed upon him. Do you not find that somewhat strange? What do you make of it Watson?"

"I suppose it IS a bid odd, but more likely the dog was responding merely to the squire's voice. Wait a moment, now Shadow's ears are twitching and it's looking in the direction of the front hallway."

No sooner had the words been spoken than a knock was heard at the door, followed by a brief commotion. Barrymore soon entered, followed quickly by Sergeant Bullfinch, who spoke with a worried look on his face. Something was terribly wrong.

"Sir Henry, gentlemen, I apologize for interrupting you so early in the morning, but I fear I have a serious problem on my hands and I am here to ask your help. Please let me explain. Very early this morning, Mrs. Estabrook, Mr. Frankland's house-keeper, arrived breathless at the police station. It seems that upon her arrival for work this morning at Lafter Hall, she could not locate Mr. Frankland.

Furthermore, she stated that when she searched the second floor she noticed that his bed had not been slept in. It was Mrs. Estabrook's understanding that Mr. Frankland was to have had dinner with you here at Baskerville Hall last night, Sir Henry. Is that correct?"

The baronet replied with great concern. Why, yes, sergeant. I'm sorry to say that he left earlier than expected, and in a foul mood. I offered to have Perkins drive him home, but he would have nothing of it."

"I see; about what time was that, Sir Henry?"

The baronet looked over to Holmes and Watson for support. "Well, I believe that it was close to 10 PM as I recall. What now, gentlemen?"

Bullfinch spoke in earnest. "Mr. Holmes, I would be obliged if I could count on your help in this matter, seeing as how you and the doctor are already here and all."

Holmes nodded. "Always happy to assist the local author-ities, sergeant. By the way, was not Mr. Frankland previously burned in effigy by the townsfolk of Fernworthy for a legal matter that went against them?"

"Now that you mention it, yes. He was able to get the woods closed where they liked to picnic on Sundays. The residents were truly up in arms, they were. Mr. Holmes, you don't think…"

"I was just stating a fact, sergeant. I would suggest that you check in with the police there. I trust that you have already made more local contact with the authorities in Coombe Tracey?"

Bullfinch nodded in affirmation, but the name Coombe Tracey jolted the squire. Laura needed to be told about her father's disappearance. He wondered how she would receive the news given their strained relationship. Holmes seemed to read the squires thoughts.

"Sir Henry, we leave it to you to update Laura on the sudden disappearance of her father. While the sergeant gets the word to the outlying districts of the disappearance, Dr. Watson and I will follow the route that Mr. Frankland would have taken from here to Lafter Hall. Is there but one way sergeant?"

Bullfinch replied matter of factly. "If one is sober, Mr. Holmes."

"Excellent. Mr. Frankland was in full possession of his faculties when he departed, so we can study the road he purportedly took with a fair amount of confidence. But we must act quickly Watson, before other moorland folk inadvertently damage valuable clues in their own travels. Let us be off then gentleman to our own tasks, and good luck to all."

In a matter of minutes Holmes and Watson were walking the route that Frankland had made use of the night before. The detective's head darted in all directions in an effort to find some small clue to the current mystery, while the doctor kept his view strictly confined to the roadbed itself.

"This is becoming a dirty business Watson. I seriously doubt that we shall find Mr. Frankland alive at this juncture."

"Isn't that a bit premature Holmes, even for you? Perhaps Frankland turned an ankle walking in the dark and is waiting for help to pass by at this very moment. It rained heavily a few nights before, and these roads do not drain well. I have only seen one set of footprints thus far, and they are leading away from the hall, so they must be his."

"Bravo Watson. I see that you have put my methods of observation to good use. Let us continue on our way. If we are to find this man at all, it will be in the light of day. Hmm, I can only wonder what Mrs. Lyons was doing last night."

Watson shot him a glance. "Holmes, you can't imagine that Laura had anything to do with her father's disappearance. It's absurd."

"I don't imagine it, Watson, but if Sergeant Bullfinch is the man I believe him to be, he'll be knocking at Mrs. Lyons door sometime in the very near future. Consider this for a moment if you will. There was bad blood between Laura and her father; they were estranged. She is set to marry Sir Henry and lead a life of leisure, but in fact she will OWN nothing. Now…should her father DIE, then she would inherit his estate. People have been murdered for far less, Watson."

The doctor remained unconvinced. "I see what you mean, but I still can't bring myself to believe that…Holmes! Look, just up ahead in the middle of the road. It looks like a small patch of some reddish mixture."

The pair ran over and bent over the spot as Watson put his thumb and forefinger into the substance. He brought up a small amount, rubbed it between his fingers, and then gave it a sniff. Watson looked intently at his partner.

"Why, it's blood, Holmes. This must have been the spot where Frankland was attacked."

The detective was unconvinced. "I don't see any other foot-prints around this area. Had there been a scuffle, the surrounding roadbed would have been disturbed with other footprints as well. Let us investigate a bit more closely and...look Watson. Notice that stone protruding about three paces before the blood? Frankland tripped over it in the dark, lost his balance and hit the ground hard, there's no doubt about it."

Watson was impressed. "I believe you may be right, Holmes. But where is Frankland now?"

"We will find THAT out as we continue our journey towards Lafter Hall. You learned a great deal about the moor while you were here previously. What is that up ahead"

The doctor thought long and hard. "I recollect now; that is called Vixen Tor, and it has quite a colorful history. It seems that at one time long ago a witch..."

"No fairy tales now, please Watson. I only wanted to know it as a map reference for later on. Let us pick up the pace and keep our eyes peeled. We may yet discover what occurred last night. But the blood is a bad sign."

The pair made their way slowly up the road. The footprints became chaotic, almost frantic in their placement. Holmes shook his head and pursed his lips. Even Watson surmised that this was not going to end well. Finally, the footprints strayed off the road directly towards a wide bog near the edge of the tor.

"Watson, I am afraid that we are not going to see Mr. Frankland again, at least not in this life. See where the footprints make their way? That is why the old man did not return home last night."

The doctor turned away in disgust. "What a horrible way to die, Holmes...alone in the dark, flailing about with no one to hear his cries for help. It's positively ghastly. But I don't understand. Frankland lived on the moor these many years. He knew the country better than most, even in the dark. How could he possibly have made such a terrible mistake?"

"There's a high probability that he suffered some type of head injury in his trip and fall, Watson, and it quickly got worse as he staggered on. Had we seen other footprints, I would have sworn that we were on the right track in finally solving this case. Once again, there is a strange occurrence and Sir Henry can be tied in with it."

Watson was displeased with Holmes' choice of words. "What do you mean Sir Henry is TIED in? This is not his fault, and I don't see how he can be associated with this accident in any shape or form."

Holmes stopped in his tracks, and his voice had a tinge of annoyance to it. "I'm surprised that you do not comprehend what is happening, Watson. It's right there in front of you to see. Let us review yet AGAIN, shall we? Sir Henry's carriage loses a wheel and is nearly upended with disastrous consequences. The squire passes by a tor and is very nearly crushed by falling rock. His cousin, the next in line for the Baskerville fortune, is murdered by an intruder in his own house."

Watson's eyes begin to widen as his friend continues. "Sir Henry is himself waylaid in London coming to see us. His friend's wife, in perfect health, is found dead in her bedroom of a heart attack. And finally, his neighbor, Mr. Frankland, dies in a bog on the moor.

This is much like a shooting gallery, Watson, and Sir Henry is the bull's eye in the center of the target. The shooter keeps missing his mark, catching the periphery, but sooner or later, when we least expect it, the fiend will succeed, if we do not root him out first."

"I see your reasoning Holmes, but could not Mrs. Mortimer's and Mr. Frankland's deaths be considered merely dreadful incidences?"

"I hope to clear up Mrs. Mortimer's death shortly, Watson. Last night I spoke privately with Mr. Mortimer, and I persuaded him to allow us permission to examine the bedroom. It has remained shuttered since her death, and no one has entered since.

But that is for later. We must return now to the hall. Sergeant Bullfinch should be made aware of this situation at once, and poor Sir Henry must compound his original story to Laura of her father's disappearance with that of his death."

Watson became angry. "Where in God's name is this villain Holmes? Where is he hiding, and why can't we identify him? This is maddening. The more we stumble about..."

"Yes, I know...then more people will die. I have a theory Watson, but I don't want to divulge it until we have had a chance to inspect that bedroom. What we need is for this scoundrel to make a mistake. I only hope that happens soon. Let us be off."

Holmes was right. Sir Henry shouldered a heavy burden in telling Laura of her father's death. Back in Coombe Tracey, she sobbed quietly into his shoulder as her held her gently.

"Oh Henry. I thought that our union would bring him back to me in time, but time was something that we did not have. However cruel he was to me, I could not wish such a death on him or anyone in the world. Mr. Holmes is certain of this?"

"Yes my dear, there is little doubt. If only your father had allowed me to have Perkins drive him home...but he was such a stubborn man."

"Where is Mr. Holmes now? I wish to speak to him."

"He has gone to James' house to inspect the room where Catherine died. He believes that he may yet find a clue to tie in all of these events, although at this point...I just don't know."

He hugged her tightly and spoke with a hint of resignation. "I'm beginning to lose hope Laura."

Watson was of the same mindset. As he knocked on the front door to the Mortimer residence, he revealed his own innermost thoughts. "I'm sorry to say that I'm beginning to lose hope Holmes. This is like a nightmare that will not end."

The great detective was undeterred. "Do not despair; I will not rest until I have secured the safety of the last of the Baskervilles...or IS he?"

Before Watson could reply to that intriguing question, the door opened and they were met by Mortimer himself. He face looked drawn and worn out. It was obvious that his wife's death was weighing heavily upon him, although he had managed to put up a brave front to those around him, as he disdained pity.

"Good afternoon, gentlemen; thank you for coming. I presented my housekeeper with a surprise holiday, and she eagerly accepted it. I thought that it would be best if you had privacy during your...investigation. Won't you come this way?"

The doctor tried to keep his emotions in check, but as they climbed the stairs and stopped before the locked bedroom door, he let out a long sigh and his shoulders dropped noticeably. This was not going to be easy for him. He reached into his vest pocket and fished out a skeleton key, which he gently placed in the door lock and turned it slowly to the left.

The mechanism made a slight clicking sound, then Mortimer turned the knob and opened the door to what he now must have considered a death chamber. Only the fading light of an approaching sunset made its way through the bedroom window, giving off an eerie glow. He stepped in quietly, as did Holmes and Watson. It was as quiet as an empty church, and the air was just as heavy.

Holmes glanced quickly about the room and focused immediately on the bed. "Mr. Mortimer, you stated that no one has touched this room since your wife's demise, and yet the bed is made. Why is that?"

"The answer is simple, Mr. Holmes. Catherine died before turning down the covers. She was found over here on the floor, lying…face up clutching her chest." He turned his head and looked away. Watson came forward and put his hand on the man's shoulder.

Holmes was less inclined to offer condolences. He walked slowly around the room, inspecting everything that crossed his path. Nothing seemed out of the ordinary, and it was then he spotted it, lying on top of a bureau. His eyes widened as he clapped his hands together and turned quickly to Mortimer.

"My good sir…the butterfly; this may appear insignificant, but do you know where it was when the housekeeper entered the room and discovered your wife's body? I realize that you were on holiday, but the police must have given you some particulars upon your return."

Mortimer was puzzled. "Why, yes, Mr. Holmes. The insect was right on the bureau as you see it now. It must have come through the window and died from a lack of nourishment and water. Catherine loved butterflies very much. I'm sure that she would have been thrilled at such a find; it is so rare."

The detective stepped towards the bureau. "What do you mean by rare; in what way?"

"Why, that is a Marsh Frittilary, Mr. Holmes. I can tell by the wings, that is, the tri colored pattern…orange, brown, and white. They are normally only found in the Great Grimpen Mire. I know this because Stapleton was fond of frequently showing off the latest specimens to his butterfly collection whenever we would dine at Merripit House."

Holmes looked confidently at his partner; although Watson was still in the dark as to the meaning of this disclosure, he knew full well what the expression on Holmes' face meant; THE vital clue to the case had been uncovered at last.

Holmes took out his handkerchief, gingerly picked up the butterfly, and then slowly brought it up to his face. He took a whiff and shook his head. "Watson, please come here and tell me what you smell."

Although skeptical, Watson did as he was told, and then the truth hit him. "I would state confidently for the record that this specimen still has the very faint odor of bitter almonds."

Mortimer grew apprehensive. "Bitter almonds? What does that mean to you gentlemen?"

Watson hesitated for a moment, but then blurted out a reply. "You as a doctor should know this, my good man. Bitter almond smell is a classic sign of…cyanide poisoning."

Holmes cut in. "Your wife was deliberately murdered, Mr. Mortimer; most probably as a way to lure Sir Henry back to Baskerville Hall, but it was also revenge."

Mortimer was astonished. "REVENGE, Mr. Holmes? What could Catherine have done to cause someone to kill her? She was such a gentle soul."

"But YOU brought ME here to the moor to aid the new baronet after the sudden death of Sir Charles and upset his plans."

"HIS plans? Who do you mean Holmes?"

"I mean Jack Stapleton, the first cousin of Sir Henry, and by the way, the one still next in line to the Baskerville fortune. He did NOT die in the mire as we all suspected. He somehow survived and is directing these horrible events even as we speak."

Mortimer was still not convinced. "But Catherine had a heart attack."

Watson shook his head no. "Think man; cyanide bonds with the hemoglobin in the blood stream. This prevents oxidation of the blood cells and one essentially dies of asphyxiation.

The coroner's report stated that she was found clutching her chest. Catherine did not have a massive heart attack; in actuality... she was struggling for breath due to the poison. She inhaled the cyanide, but it also entered her body dermally through the skin of her hands. That twofold combination was quick and lethal."

Mortimer swayed for a moment, and then slumped into a sitting position on the bed. "I can scarcely believe it. Stapleton still alive. Then not only Sir Henry...but ALL of us are in mortal danger."

Holmes looked out the window. "Everything points to Stapleton, but I don't believe that he is orchestrating this all by himself. He is sure to have a trusty confederate, possibly several of them."

Watson began to pace the room. "Then we must root him out. If we know where he is, then it should be simple enough to..."

Mortimer was not as optimistic. "No, it's NOT as simple as it sounds, doctor. The Grimpen Mire is vast and impassable. We don't know his entry and exit points, we cannot surround it with police, and there is no one alive, other than Stapleton himself, who still knows how to get in and about without being sucked down into its depths. He is safe within an impenetrable fortress of rock, soft turf, and sludge, I am sorry to say."

Holmes was not deterred. "Nevertheless, we now know that the villain Stapleton is most probably alive...and that HE is the cause of the bedlam surrounding Sir Henry. Forewarned is forearmed gentlemen, and unless I miss my guess, Mr. Frankland's death is not so cut and dry a situation after all."

Watson spoke with a determined tone. "How do we root the blaggard out Holmes? What do we do next?"

Holmes stopped to think. "Stapleton does not yet know that we are on to him; this gives us the advantage...at least for the moment. Let us return to Baskerville Hall and give Sir Henry the bad news that his delightful relation is still among the living. We must keep a watchful eye on the baronet day and night, at least from a respectable distance."

Mortimer protested. "I must say that I don't like your choice of words, Mr. Holmes. It almost sounds as though you are planning to use Henry as bait to draw Stapleton out."

"That is what I plan to do, sir, although the exact circumstances required to do this safely are not yet formulated. One thing is certain...if that dog is as loyal as it appears, the baronet's kindness is about to be rewarded."

CHAPTER 14

A Trio Of Conspirators

Murphy sat uncomfortably on the front seat of his cart, occasionally snapping the reigns in an attempt to coax a bit more effort from the horse pulling it along the road that paralleled the great Grimpen Mire. The night air had a distinct chill that made him shudder; his overcoat was proving insufficient, and that irritated him. He mumbled under his breath but continued on until he reached the site that he desired, then pulled on the reigns until the cart came to a halt just on the outer edge of the lane.

And there he waited patiently in the darkness; for how long he did not know. The crickets and night birds of the moor serenaded him to the point where he nearly drifted off to sleep. Just as his eyes began to close he heard the rustling sound of approaching footsteps from the mire. He was fairly confident of the person's identity, but he was not a gambling man.

"Who's out there? Identify yourself."

The reply was cheerful and reassuring. "Very good, Murphy; very good indeed. You are proving to be quite the capable assistant. No use taking any chances with that meddlesome Sherlock Holmes lurking about the countryside. I trust that you have brought my provisions? I was running low."

"As you ordered, Mr. Stapleton. I have water, some tins of food, more blankets, another goat for HER, and some very interesting news for you to mull over, and believe me, you WILL want to know about this."

Stapleton's enthusiasm quickly vanished in a flash. "And just what is this INTERESTING NEWS that you speak of?" His eyes began to glow.

Murphy hopped off and made his way to the back of the cart, carefully offloading the supplies into his master's outstretched arms. "Old man Frankland is dead; at least that's what everyone believes. He left Baskerville Hall after dinner the other night and was never seen again. Sherlock Holmes discovered his trail the next day, and his footsteps led directly to a bog...near her tor."

Stapleton became enraged. "DAMN HER! She was given explicit instructions to stay hidden and do nothing until ordered by us. Can you control this witch or not?"

Murphy was caught off guard momentarily by the severe tone of Stapleton's question. "I sensed that she was becoming restless, but why are you so upset? This has nothing to do with us, and we are not certain that it was her doing."

Stapleton spewed out his reply. "Are you a simpleton? This comes at exactly the wrong time for us. The local police can be easily fooled, but Sherlock Holmes will not view this as an accident; to him it will be yet another suspicious death. There will be even more scrutiny, something we must avoid if we are to succeed. Finish helping me get these items into the mine, and then we will go to see the bitch."

Murphy was not finished. "Oh, but there is more. Whilst in Grimpen today I chanced to pass some women talking in the village square. It seems that Sir Henry and Laura Lyons...are going to be married."

Stapleton was shocked. "MARRIED? TO LAURA LYONS? Why, that does create an interesting set of circumstances. I will use this new love against him as I did with my wife. It will be of little bother to snatch and bring her to the moor. She will be the bait that entices my cousin to us. He dare not refuse."

Murphy followed close behind Stapleton as they made their way along the hidden path through the great Grimpen Mire to the old tin mine. One false step would have the gypsy up to his waist in muck, so he placed his foot in each spot that his master had just vacated. It was an unsettling trip in the light of day, but the near darkness made it terrifying. Finally, they reached the entrance to the mine, and Murphy took a deep breath of relief. Stapleton heard him and was amused.

"Why do you worry so? I know this way like the back of my hand."

Murphy was at a loss. "But HOW Jack? The old stake markers you used before to guide your way are gone. You ripped them up yourself."

Stapleton shook his head in agreement. "That is true; when my plan to kill Sir Henry failed, I was forced to remove them up as I made my way back to the safety of the mine, otherwise that meddlesome Holmes would have followed my trail. I had a devil of a time finding it once again, especially since I had to work in the dark so that I would not be seen, but I accomplished my task, as you can see. Now, into the mine with these supplies."

The ride to the tor was fairly quiet. Murphy knew that Stapleton was thinking long and hard, and the gypsy dared not break his master's concentration. Only the occasional bleating of the goat tied up in the back of the cart broke the silence. Finally, they arrived at the tor. Before either of them could hop off the cart, they heard a woman's voice from above.

"Ah, my saviors are here. What have you come for this time?"

Murphy retrieved the goat and carried it to the base of the tor, while Stapleton decided to bring up the rear. "I bring your supper, Vixiana, but we also come for answers."

The old witch cackled with delight. "Ask what you will. Shall I answer with a riddle?"

Stapleton was in no mood for such banter. "Enough of this claptrap. Was it you who killed Mr. Frankland the other night?"

Vixiana spun around the top of the tor with her hands outstretched as Murphy quickly put a hand under his shirt to grasp the amulet Syeira had given him. "Shall I tell you how the old man died? At first, he did not understand what was happening in the fog; then, as he sunk lower into the bog, the reality of his plight began to set in and he thrashed about like a great fish caught in a net.

He begged me to help him while my laughter filled the air. At the end, his eyes pleaded with me after his mouth and nose had sunk under…and the deed was nearly done. Finally, his arms and hands stopped waving to and fro, and even they sunk below the mire. How sweet a sight after so many years."

Murphy was repulsed and said nothing, but Stapleton was not one to let a calamity go to waste, sociopath that he was. "Vixiana, do you desire to witness more scenes like that…and on a regular basis? If you do, then I have a proposal that you may appreciate. All you need do is kill Sir Henry Baskerville, and we shall release you from your servitude in perpetuity."

Vixiana's face beamed with joy. "A Baskerville… a Baskerville STILL LIVES! I have not heard that name since Sir Hugo was torn to shreds by the hound of hell. Many were the times we reveled in evil together, Squire Hugo and I."

Stapleton was taken aback. He was not sure that he had heard correctly. "The hound of hell? What are you TALKING about? Are you telling us that there really WAS such a creature on the moor?"

Vixiana spewed out her reply with disdain. "Of course there was a hound, you fool! Why do you find it so strange that I could exist...but not poor Sir Hugo's dog of death? Now speak to me further about...ending my servitude."

Stapleton saw that he had piqued her interest as expected. "It is as I said, kill the Baskerville, and you shall be free. It is really quite simple. We will deliver him to you in the evening hours, and then you can deal with him in your usual way. There is only one provision. I must be present when he dies. I too wish to revel in his agony. Now do we have a deal?"

Vixiana hooted with delight. "Yes, yes, we have...a deal, as you call it. Bring me the Baskerville, and it shall be done. But we must seal our pact in blood. Bring the goat to my cave and we shall finalize our bargain."

Murphy hauled the bleating goat inside. The hollow was a stinking mess of bones and hanging entrails. Both men began to gag but stayed nonetheless. Vixiana swung the rope over a wooden cross beam and pulled the goat into the air while its feet flailed piteously.

With one swift stroke of her long nails, she slit the beast's throat and began cupping the blood into her hands. When she had drawn enough, the witch then proceeded to coat her hands with the warm sticky liquid until they resembled scarlet claws. She motioned each of them towards her. Reluctantly, the men came forward and the three shook hands in blood.

Vixiana was satisfied. "The pact is complete. Now bring me the Baskerville!"

The ride back to the tin mine was a study in contrasts. While Stapleton was content with the bargain he had made with Vixiana, his partner Murphy was far less satisfied, and it showed in his tone.

"You should NOT have given her such a proposition without my consent. Once she regains her freedom, my gypsies will be at great risk, along with any other unsuspecting travelers on the moor. If I can manage to keep her under my control, she can be of great use to me and my people."

Stapleton rose from his hiding place among the hay bales in the back of the cart, and he remained defiant. "Never forget who is in charge, Murphy. I decide what course of action to follow in this endeavor. My neck is squarely in the noose should we be uncovered. And in case you were not aware, you are an accessory to these crimes, and will therefore suffer the same fate."

His voice softened ever so slightly. "Besides, when all of this is over, you will not need her help, for you will be a rich man, free to go anywhere you choose. Remember that it was the gypsies who rejected YOU and your family long ago. They do not warrant a second thought."

That reminded Murphy of the uneasy deal that had been brokered. "And you remember our agreement, Stapleton; I am to receive 40% of the inheritance…and not a shilling less; that is my share."

Jack smiled, but Murphy did not notice. "I have not forgotten. You will receive just reward for your efforts…depend upon it. But now it grows late; take me back to the mine. And now that the final leg of this black journey is under way, I am certain the great Sherlock Holmes can sense that the finale is close at hand. The question remains…can he plan ahead to checkmate my moves? He must know that Sir Henry is in serious trouble."

The following morning, a haggard looking Holmes stood pacing back and forth on the creaky wooden platform of Oakhampton Station.

Watson sat passively on a nearby bench observing his every move. He knew better than to interrupt his partner when he was in such a state, so he sat back, took a deep breath of air, and waited. Finally, Holmes stopped in his tracks and spoke to him in great earnest.

"Watson, Henry Baskerville is in serious trouble, and up to this point, I must admit that I have been unable to help him. However, I have a strong feeling that this nightmare shall come to a close very soon. Whether it is a successful conclusion remains to be seen. Both the baronet's life and my reputation….hello, here we are."

A split second later the arriving 7:05 train screamed its shrill whistle of announcement from around a slight bend and steamed slowly into the station. Shortly after coming to a complete stop, the coach doors opened wide and a slew of passengers began to exit onto the platform from adjoining cars.

The foot traffic was unusually heavy, so much so that at first Holmes could not find his intended mark. Finally, he spied a black bowler hat bobbing up and down amidst the throng and waived his hand in the air. The owner of the hat took notice and went straight towards him.

Watson acknowledged his own disbelief. "I never thought I'd be happy to see HIM sniffing about one of our active investigations, but I must admit…we need help."

Holmes let out a loud, hasty laugh at the irony of the situation. "I heartily agree Watson, but we must focus on the bigger picture here, and that, of course, is Sir Henry. Now put your pride in your pocket and at least please TRY to be cordial."

As the man in the bowler approached, Holmes extended his hand in friendship. "Hello Lestrade. Thank you for coming on such short notice. I trust that you had a pleasant trip from London?"

The Scotland Yarder was caught off guard for a moment, and he quickly eyed both men with suspicion, which brought them some amusement. This was not the Sherlock Holmes that he had grown accustomed to over the years, and he was suddenly uncomfortable.

"Ahh...why...yes, Mr. Holmes. I left the Yard as soon as I received your telegram, and in all honesty, it was very short on details, I must say; but I knew that if YOU were requesting MY help that it must be important. What is this all about, bringing me back here to Dartmoor?"

Holmes brow furrowed. "Just an enduring case of murder Lestrade, and it all centers around our old friend, Henry Baskerville."

Lestrade exploded. "THE SQUIRE? But...but...that case is closed Mr. Holmes. Stapleton and his hound are dead. You shot the dog, and Stapleton died in the Great Grimpen Mire."

Watson shook his head in agreement. "That was our previous assessment too, but bad things have been happening on the moor lately."

Holmes ushered Lestrade off the platform and through the station house. Just up the road a bit Perkins waited patiently with the coach from the hall. He hopped down from his perch and opened the coach door as the three men climbed inside.

As they slowly made their way back to Dartmoor, Holmes brought Lestrade up to snuff as to the events that had taken place since his return to London with Sergeant Bleeker and Beryl Stapleton. The inspector became visibly dismayed as Holmes furnished him with the updated events surrounding Sir Henry and those close to him.

"Blimey, Mr. Holmes, this is not the open and shut case that we were led to believe. There are just too many unfortunate circumstances taking place in succession for this all to be bad luck. Do you have a theory as to who is ultimately behind all this?"

Holmes' eyes narrowed. "There can only be one culprit behind all this, Lestrade. Jack Stapleton is still alive and acting as the grand master on this peculiar chess board of ours. There is no other reasonable explanation. He is in hiding, with a trusted confederate to aid him in fulfilling his plan to kill Sir Henry and inherit the Baskerville fortune."

Lestrade could not object. "Well strike me up a gum tree, but I have to agree with you, Mr. Holmes. What do you propose that we do now?"

Holmes exhaled and looked vacantly out the carriage window. "It would be obvious to say that we must protect Sir Henry day and night, but doing that would be simply a false sense of accomplishment. Time is on the side of this fiend Stapleton. He knows full well that we cannot stay and guard the baronet indefinitely."

Watson threw his hands in the air in frustration. "Dash it all, Holmes, what are we to do then? Are you saying that we should NOT guard Sir Henry?"

Lestrade caught on to Holmes' train of thought and raised his eyebrows in disbelief. "Now wait just a minute, Mr. Holmes. I hope you're not suggesting that we...that we..." He could not finish the sentence.

Holmes was emphatic in his reply. "I AM most definitely suggesting it. Lestrade. We must use Sir Henry as BAIT in order to draw this villain out into the open once and for all."

Watson could not comprehend what he had just heard. "You must be joking, Holmes. If we were to implement this plan and something were to happen to the baronet, well, it would be a stain on us all. You are gambling with Sir Henry's life."

Holmes would not relent. "Yes, we ARE gambling, Watson, but we are gambling to SAVE Sir Henry's life; if we were to do otherwise, Stapleton would succeed sooner or later. It is an unsettling probability. Fortunately, we have Lestrade with us now to bolster our cause. By the by, inspector, are you willing to put yourself at my disposal?"

Lestrade shifted uncomfortably in his seat and forced himself to put on a brave face that quickly brought on a remark dripping with sarcasm. "Why...of course, Mr. Holmes. I wouldn't have it any other way. You have the advantage of me under these circumstances, having stayed on the case as it were...AFTER you assured me that it was CLOSED."

Watson became red-faced and immediately opened his mouth as if to reply, but Holmes shot him a glance and he remained silent; however, the good doctor's lips moved with a noiseless reply, asserting if only to himself what he really wanted to say. Whether the inspector realized it or not, Lestrade had just dodged a stinging verbal bullet aimed directly at his most vulnerable spot—his ego.

Not surprisingly, the remainder of the trip was without dialogue of any kind, and the silence only seemed to intensify a feeling of awkwardness. Finally, the carriage pulled up to the entrance of Baskerville Hall, and Perkins completed his morning's task by opening the coach door for his passengers. As Lestrade sauntered his way up the walk, he was met at the front door by the squire, who shook his hand enthusiastically.

"Inspector Lestrade, how good to see you, and thank you for coming back to Dartmoor once again to help me. I am sorry to have to take you away from more pressing matters in London, but as I'm sure Mr. Holmes and Dr. Watson have informed you, it would appear that I require further assistance."

Lestrade nodded in appreciation, and then puffed up like a proud peacock. "Nothing is more pressing than a case of murder, Sir Henry. Scotland Yard is always happy to help pull Sherlock Holmes' chestnuts out of the fire. After all, he has helped me once or twice in the past."

Watson was now apoplectic, but his anger was instantly diffused by Holmes' laughter. Sir Henry sensed what was happening and made good use of his duties as host.

"Won't you please come in, gentlemen? I have a bit of a problem on my hands at this very moment and I may require ALL of you to intercede for me."

The trio glanced at one another and followed Sir Henry into the drawing room. Sitting by the fire was Laura Lyons, with Shadow lying down beside her like the great sphinx of Egypt. The dog raised its head, sniffed the air and glared at Lestrade, who stopped dead in his tracks with fear before speaking.

"SUFFERING CATS, Mr. Holmes, you didn't tell me about this...this...THING!"

Watson was quite pleased with the situation. "So sorry old boy, but in our haste to fill you in about all of the unfortunate events swirling around Sir Henry of late, we neglected to tell you about a fortunate one. Say hello to Shadow, the squire's newest bodyguard...and faithful companion, I might add."

Shadow popped up at the sight of a stranger and slowly circled Lestrade, much to the baronet's delight. The inspector stood straight as an arrow without movement of any kind. Whether he was frozen in fear or merely displaying good judgment could not be confirmed with a fair amount of certainty. Finally, the dog lost all interest and sidled up to Sir Henry, who patted him gently on the head. Lestrade in turn breathed a sigh of relief. Holmes could not help but make light of the situation.

"Well, Sir Henry, now that it appears everyone has been properly introduced, perhaps you can be so kind as to reveal to us the source of your NEWEST problem. I trust that it is not too serious."

While all eyes focused on the baronet, it was Laura who spoke up with a faltering voice. "I'm very sorry, gentlemen, but it looks as if I am the source of the newest problem."

CHAPTER 15

Close Call At Vixen Tor

T he drawing room suddenly grew still. No one could believe what Laura had just said, except for the baronet of course, and his expression gave away no details. Finally, Watson began to chuckle before speaking up.

"My dear, I must admit that you certainly had us all fooled for a moment. How could YOU possibly be the source of another dilemma for us? We are all thrilled about your present AND future relationship with Sir Henry. I just don't understand."

Laura stood up wringing her hands and faced them. "I must speak plainly then. It will of course come as no shock to anyone here that my father and I were estranged. He was mortified that the family name would be shamed by me, a married woman living apart from her husband. The more he protested, the more stubborn I became, especially since he did not approve of the union to begin with. Ultimately, a complete break was inevitable."

The inspector cut in clumsily. "I understand completely, Mrs. Lyons. My old dad and I used to have terrible rows, and then one day..."

Holmes summarily cut him off. "LESTRADE! Please continue Laura."

"Well, when Henry told me about…how he…died, I knew that not only would there be no reconciliation between us, but there would be no wake, no church service, not even a grave to visit. So I am determined to go the spot on the moor where he died…to the bog that pulled him under. I feel that this is my duty to perform as his daughter, and I am going today."

Watson was about to reply, but Sir Henry put up his hand. "Please, gentlemen, believe me when I say that there is no dissuading her in this matter. Furthermore, as Laura's future husband, I feel that I should be by her side in this ordeal. Now perhaps you understand my newest problem, doctor."

Watson reluctantly agreed. "I most certainly do, Sir Henry, and in all honesty I must say that you are both making a rash decision. Surely you must realize that this will be a dangerous undertaking under the present circumstances. We have no way of knowing where or when your adversary may strike, so…"

Holmes finished the sentence; "So WE must then take the proper counter measures to insure the safety of you both, and this is how it will be accomplished. It does involve an element of risk, but we may just be able to draw our opponent into the light of day and apprehend him. Is there anyone who objects?"

Watson began to say something, but stopped. Lestrade clasped his hands together uneasily but did not reply either. Finally, the baronet and his lady looked at each other and stayed silent. Holmes grew excited; the game was afoot.

"EXCELLENT! Sir Henry, you and Laura shall leave here after luncheon, say…3PM. That will give Lestrade time to round up Sergeant Bullfinch; leaving from Lafter Hall, they will be able to position themselves at a discreet distance near the fateful bog. Watson and I shall trail Laura and Sir Henry from Baskerville Hall. In that way, BOTH directions will be covered. With any luck, we may meet Stapleton and his henchman somewhere in the middle and nab them."

Lestrade seemed more amenable after this explanation, but Watson was still not sure. "But Holmes, we will need to be at a fair distance away from the couple in order for this plan to work. Time could be of the essence if there is an attack, don't you agree?"

Holmes was pleased but also surprised that the doctor had grasped the situation so clearly. "Bravo, Watson. You are absolutely correct; that is why Shadow will accompany them on their journey. Now are you satisfied?"

Watson finally yielded, but something else caught his attention. Shadow had lifted its head and stared at the detective. "Holmes, don't you think it strange that this dog knows the new name that Sir Henry has given it after only a few days? It's uncanny."

The baronet provided his own opinion. "I'm not all that knowledgeable about canines, doctor, but I don't think it's that unusual. After all, the dog had been living on its own for who knows how long. Shadow would have to be quite intelligent to have survived in such a hostile environment. Do you agree Mr. Holmes?"

But the great detective was already lost in his own thoughts. The sound of his name swiftly drew his attention back to the group. "Ahhh...I must admit that pets have never been a point of interest for me. I know nothing about their behaviors or proclivities. Suffice it to say, though, that I believe Shadow to be an admirable bodyguard for both you and Laura at this juncture.

Lestrade, if you would be so kind as to go to the village and enlist the aid of Sergeant Bullfinch, I believe that our trap will have an auspicious beginning. Sir Henry, could it be possible for Perkins to convey Lestrade to Grimpen, and then afterwards back out to Merripit House? It would arouse less suspicion, as he and the sergeant could hunker down in the carriage."

The squire readily agreed. "Of course, Mr. Holmes; I will see to it at once. If you would all excuse me, I will go and check on the arrangements."

As Sir Henry left the room, Holmes focused his attention on Laura. "My dear, you do realize that you are taking a potentially gave risk in this endeavor?"

She did not disagree, but remained firm in her conviction. "I realize the danger for both Henry and me, Mr. Holmes, but it simply is something that I must do. And I am sorry for the inconvenience, but I am convinced that as long as Shadow is with us, we will come to no harm."

The dog stared at Holmes as though waiting for a reply, but none came. The rest of the morning was pleasant enough, with the squire and Laura discussing their future plans together, while Holmes and Watson waited patiently in the great room for Lestrade and Bullfinch to arrive from Grimpen.

After a light luncheon of bread, fruit and cheese provided by Mrs. Barrymore, the group was ready to follow the plan that had been agreed upon. Perkins brought the carriage around to the back of the hall, and after the two policemen scampered into the coach, made straight for Lafter Hall.

Holmes took out his pocket watch. "We will give them roughly 15 minutes to arrive at Lafter Hall, after which Perkins will return alone. There they will have 5 minutes to look the place over, and then another 20 to walk their way back towards the bog. They will be watching for any suspicious activity along the way, so we can be assured that direction is clear of any dangers.

Sir Henry, in one half-hours' time, you and Laura...plus Shadow of course, may depart from the hall. Watson and I will follow at a discreet distance. The dog will provide you with immediate protection, while Watson and I will protect your rear. I believe that covers everything."

The next 30 minutes felt like 30 hours to the young couple, but the chosen time finally arrived and they ventured out hand in hand onto the road and Shadow led the way. There was very little in the way of conversation, with the great hound venturing ahead some 10 meters but no more. Finally, they grew near to the bog, and the squire indicated their proximity by drawing Laura to his side and putting his arm over her shoulder.

She knew what that meant. Her body stiffened and she began to take short breaths. As they rounded a curve, the bog lay before them off to the side of the road. Shadow instinctively stayed well enough away. The dog was well aware of the danger, and he whined an alarm for his master as the two approached.

Laura responded. "No need to worry, good Shadow; we will stay clear. So this is the spot. Oh Henry, what a horrible way to die...helpless and alone in the darkness. As cruel as he was to me, I would not wish such an end on anyone."

She buried her head in his shoulder and began to cry. The squire said nothing, preferring to let his lady vent her anguish all at once. Finally, after she had shed her bitter tears, Laura drew a red rose from her coat pocket and tossed it onto the murky bog. She drew solace from the fact that it did not sink below the surface.

"My mother loved roses. She grew them in her garden and along the front of the house. Father always pretended to pay them no mind, but he was proud of them, too. After she died, he would get up early in the morning and tend to them. He didn't want me to know, but I woke up early one day and there he was, pruning them carefully in the dawn light. And now...they are both gone."

Henry spoke up. "No, my dear; now they are TOGETHER. I will have a headstone with his name put nearby. He will not be forgotten, believe me. If we are done here, I suggest..."

The baronet's words were cut short by Shadow, who raised his hackles and began to growl ominously in the direction of nearby Vixen Tor. A scant few seconds later, a loud, hideous wail filled the air and then subsided. Laura threw her arms around Henry in sheer terror.

"OH MY GOD. What was that sound Henry? It was…it was…unearthly."

The squire did not want to let on that he was just as terrified. "I have heard the local farmers say that when moor ponies stray into the bogs, they can make horrible sounds in their death agonies. That must have been what it was.

Laura, you have made your peace with your father. Now let us return to the hall before it grows dark. I must see to the comfort of my guests, and the Barrymore's will need extra time to prepare."

As they were about to leave, Sir Henry glanced back for Shadow. The dog, still looking in the direction of Vixen Tor, was leaning forward as though getting ready to repel a formidable enemy. The baronet was having none of it.

"Shadow, come along boy. We are leaving."

His master's voice changed the dog's focus, and he grudgingly turned and caught up to them, occasionally stopping to sniff the air along the way. By sunset, all of the participants were back at the hall and warming themselves in front of the fireplace. The weather was growing cooler with each passing day.

Holmes stared dejectedly into the fire. "I would have wagered 100 pounds that an attempt would have been made on Sir Henry's life this day. Lestrade, you and Sergeant Bullfinch say you saw nothing unusual on your trek?"

Lestrade answered reluctantly. "That's right, Mr. Holmes. We nosed about Lafter Hall momentarily, that is, we circled the house, and then made our way in the direction of the bog as you ordered. We saw no one at all, but we did hear that high pitched shriek, or what sounded like a shriek, as we neared an adjacent tor. For a moment, we thought that might be the trouble we had expected up ahead, but then the sound abruptly stopped. Do YOU have any idea what it was?"

"We all heard it too, but couldn't locate the source. Sir Henry seems to think that it was a dying moor pony stuck in a nearby bog, although from the dog's reaction, Shadow may have his own ideas. Unfortunately, he can't talk. I'm at a loss; either Stapleton has thoroughly missed his mark, or..."

He stopped speaking and looked at Watson, who revealed his confused. "Or WHAT Holmes? What does it all mean?"

Holmes began to pace back and forth in front of the fire. "Perhaps Stapleton is not merely waiting for the squire to show himself by chance. This fiend has a grand scheme in mind that he has chosen to follow, make no mistake about it. The question is, how can we discover what it is before..."

He stopped in mid-sentence out of embarrassment, but Sir Henry finished it for him. "I know; you mean...before it's too late, Mr. Holmes. My friends, I realize that you are all doing your very best on my behalf. I have faith that Providence will somehow see us through this wretched state of affairs."

With that, Barrymore entered the room to announce that dinner was ready, signaling a brief respite for the weary group. But there was no respite for those who desired the death of the baronet. Jack Stapleton shivered within the tin mine on the great Grimpen Mire. His repast consisted of a tin of sardines and stale bread, washed down with tepid water. He sat on a large rock and pointed a dull fork at his unhappy confederate while speaking his mind.

"And I said I don't care where or when Baskerville travels about the moor, Murphy. I won't be rushed into a foolish move against the squire with that damned Sherlock Holmes lurking about, waiting to pounce. We will stick to the plan and that is my final word on the matter."

Murphy got red in the face and stamped his foot. "But if we just wait and bide our time until they give up and leave, I could take him out with one shot when he decides to goes out riding."

Stapleton snickered. "I know what you're trying to do; you want to keep control of that witch for yourself. Well, I could care less about your little scheme. Besides, my cousin's death must look like an accident, or at least a reasonable facsimile. Should the police consider his demise to be a case of murder, then even the safety of Costa Rica may not help me in acquiring my inheritance.

You see, in South America, some well-placed bribes can go a very long way in taking care of the legal protestations that will arise from England regarding my inheritance, but should homicide enter into the mix, then the situation becomes highly problematic. The authorities would not relish the idea of aiding a suspected murderer in their midst, especially one from another country. NOW do you see why we must stay the course that I have charted?"

Stapleton's logic was impeccable, but that did not matter to the hot blooded gypsy. Murphy responded with a visibly dishonest "Of course, Jack. You are the boss. I must go now before the cloud cover fades and the moon appears. Until tomorrow, then."

As the disgruntled henchman exited the mine, Stapleton watched him carefully, and then sneered before leaning back against a wooden beam. "So you wish to play games with me, eh my friend? If the situation calls for it, I can do the same. I will see that you never receive a Scotch farthing of my money."

Murphy was still dissatisfied, and he quickly made for the gypsy encampment. Once again, his arrival was not a welcome sight. Cold stares and whispers were all that he received as he halted his cart and walked straight towards Syeira's wagon barely beyond range of the firelight. Just as he was about to knock on her door, he felt a tug on his sleeve that pulled him backwards. It was one of the elders.

"Do you remember how much gypsies appreciate their camp dogs, Murphy? They are our eyes and ears. Well, the dogs have been in a bad way for several days now, growling and sniffing the air as though a terrible thing is near."

Murphy jerked his arm out of the old man's grasp and replied cautiously; "And what does that have to do with me, Gregor? I have done nothing."

The response was icy. "The dogs have been restless since the day you returned to visit with Syeira. There are people here who believe that this is not a coincidence. Why did you decide to return after so long?"

Murphy blubbered out a reply. "I need no reason to visit my own grandmother...and don't forget, I am still of gypsy blood. Perhaps someday soon you will all come to appreciate me. Now mind your business and leave me alone."

Gregor remained unconvinced. "You are hiding something, Murphy. Of that I have no doubt. Remember this...if your actions were to harm any in our band, then even Syeira would be unable to protect you; I promise."

As the old man turned to leave, one of the camp dogs howled in fear. Soon, the rest of the pack joined in, and frightened women called to their children to return to the light of the camp fire. Murphy cursed the dogs under his breath and knocked softly on the wagon door. In a few moments, Syeira opened it and waved him inside without a word being spoken. She looked both angry and distressed.

"And what brings you back here to me, my grandson? I sense that you have not followed my advice."

Murphy hardened. "No, I did not. She is in my power, but my master desires to free her after she kills the present squire at Baskerville Hall; that is a wasted opportunity. With Vixiana under my command, we can right many of the wrongs that have been done to our people in the past, and I will be welcomed back with open arms."

Syeira grew sad. "She is not one to be trusted. Do not be fooled into believing that you can ever really control such a creature. Above all else, she is a deceiver, like her TRUE master."

The old woman put her hands on his head. "Nicola, my grandson, there is something that you do not know. Vixiana was ALSO a gypsy, cast out by our band long ago because of her evil ways. This witch will never agree to support us now. In truth, just the opposite will occur. She harbored a strong hatred against those who cast her out, and time has not slackened her thirst for vengeance. You must destroy her if you truly desire our people and those on the moor to be safe once again. It is the only way."

This was not the advice that Murphy had hoped for. He barged out of the wagon without even the courtesy of a good-bye. Syeira began to cry as she watched him push his way through the angry crowd of onlookers towards his cart. Gregor reappeared and pointed a finger in the air before turning to speak to the throng.

"Listen well, all of you. I tell you now; this woman's grand-son will cause us great sorrow and misery. Do not doubt it for a moment. Syeira…for whatever he has done, you somehow helped him along the path he travels. Do you deny it? Swear on the blood of your ancestors."

She bowed her head. "No, I do not deny that I provided him the opportunity, but ultimately, that choice was his alone."

The crowd began to murmur; those in fear quickly made the Christian sign of the cross, or plucked amulets from their pockets and caressed them tenderly; others scowled in anger and spit on her wagon. Gregor raised his hands to calm them down. When finally they obliged, he asked the old woman the direct question all of them wanted answered.

"But when the day of reckoning arrives, where will the great Syeira's loyalties lie?"

CHAPTER 16

One Step Behind

It was a morning of meetings at Baskerville Hall. In the kitchen, Eliza stood waving her hands in the air, pleading with her husband to avoid the obvious solution to their problem. She tried to keep her voice down, but it was becoming increasingly difficult.

"I cannot believe that you are suggesting that we simply sneak out in the middle of the night like...like...rats deserting a sinking ship. It is positively shameful. YOUR people have lived in this house for over 100 years serving the Baskerville family, and this is how you believe it should end?"

Barrymore was more pragmatic in his reply, but it had deep conviction. "I am thinking about our best interests, which in this CURRENT situation means saving our lives. Can't you see what is happening? Even the great Sherlock Holmes has been unable to solve this mystery, and this is his second go round in Dartmoor."

He put a hand on her shoulder. "People linked in any number of ways with Sir Henry are DYING, Eliza. It started with his uncle Charles, then went to his cousin James, and now to his own friends—Catherine Mortimer, and Mr. Frankland. Who is to say that WE will not be next? How can we be certain?"

Eliza continued. "But he may need us now more than ever. It's not right."

Barrymore kept pounding away. "And what of that beast that he decided to bring back to the hall? The dog gives me the creeps I tell you. Have you seen the way it watches everyone? Its eyes follow me whenever I'm in the same room with the squire, as though he were waiting for me to make one false move."

Eliza shuddered. "I admit that I too am frightened by the sheer size of the thing, but I sense that it is somehow loyal to Sir Henry, for whatever reason. Besides, where would we go, and what would we do?"

Barrymore was surprised. "My dear, for once in our lives, we are now in a position to do as we please. I have just received this month's wages for us both, and don't forget that Sir Charles left us each 500 pounds in his will. We can move back to Dover temporarily and map out our future from there. Perhaps we could even go to America. Would you like that?"

Eliza was intrigued. "Yes...yes I would. But when should we do this?"

Barrymore was quick to reply. "The sooner the better; tonight, after they've all gone to bed. Pack a light bag; we can buy whatever else we need in Dover. Now let's finish getting the luncheon ready; they're waiting."

In the front parlor, Holmes was issuing instructions. "So we are all agreed then, gentlemen. Perkins will drive to Grimpen to pick up Sergeant Bullfinch, then he and Lestrade will be taken quietly to Merripit House. It is a probability that Stapleton, or at least his confederate, has been raiding the home for supplies. Perhaps we may be able to catch someone in the act."

He focused on Lestrade with a sly smile. "What do you say, inspector. Are you up for a little game of cat and mouse?"

Holmes already knew what Lestrade was thinking. If the Scotland Yarder could apprehend the murderer on his own, then he would not have to share the credit. It would be a fine feather in his cap, and make for interesting reading in the London papers. Perhaps even a promotion would follow.

Lestrade pretended not to be excited at this prospect, but he failed miserably. Even Watson was taken aback by his obvious insincerity. "Anything you say, Mr. Holmes. I am always at your disposal, of course."

Holmes turned to the baronet. "Sir Henry, your task today is to stay close to Baskerville Hall. I wish you and Shadow to wander the grounds as though merely going for a walk, but be sure to stay within sight of the hall. If anyone IS keeping you under surveillance, then I am certain that Shadow will be able not only to detect the scoundrel but apprehend him as well. Is that clear?"

The squire nodded soberly. "Yes, Mr. Holmes; I understand. In this instance, I am like a fishing lure in the stream enticing a trout to come and take a bite. Not very good for the nerves, I must say, but I will do as you ask."

Sir Henry looked over at the dog lying quietly in a corner of the room observing the group carefully. "What do you say Shadow old boy? Are you up for a stroll around the grounds later? I daresay I could even throw a few sticks and teach you to play fetch."

Everyone laughed at the thought of such a sight. The dog immediately sat up, cocked its head to one side and gave out one loud, booming bark. The laughter stopped at once, and only Holmes understood what had just occurred.

"Gentlemen, I believe that Shadow here has just experienced his very first sounds of laughter. You are well protected, Sir Henry; have no fear. This dog of yours is equal to any 3 of us."

The squire smiled. "I believe you are right. Where are you and Dr. Watson off to today?"

Holmes took out his pipe and proceeded to stuff it with tobacco. "There is only one other place that Stapleton can remain in hiding without being seen, and that is in the tin mine where he had previously kept his hound under wraps. If Watson and I can discover the trail he blazed to get there safely, then we've effectively got him trapped. I have no doubt."

The doctor responded rather glumly. "But it's an expansive moor, Holmes; we don't even know from which direction he took to enter the great Grimpen Mire. This will be like finding a needle in a haystack, don't you agree?"

Holmes concurred. "Watson, in this particular instance, I am forced to admit that you are absolutely correct. What I am hoping for is one small slip up by our adversary. If ever we needed a bit of luck, NOW would be the time, my friends. Ah...here comes Mr. and Mrs. Barrymore with our repast, and not a moment too soon. The good doctor has a lean and hungry look this morning."

Watson cheered up at the sight of food being placed on the dining table. "I usually don't approve when you quote Shakespeare, Holmes, and I take some slight offense to you comparing me to Cassius, but I won't deny that I am famished. I suggest that we all eat hearty and then be off to our respective tasks."

Everyone heeded Watson's advice without protest, and shortly thereafter the group split up. Within an hour's time, Perkins had driven Lestrade and Sergeant Bullfinch to within a quarter mile of Merripit House, where he halted the carriage and called out to his passengers.

"Excuse me, gentlemen, but Mr. Holmes directed me to stop the carriage just before we rounded this bend and the house comes into view."

Lestrade was peeved. "It's a nuissance walk to the house. Are you sure that these are Mr. Holmes' instructions?"

Perkins responded carefully. "Mr. Holmes was of the opinion that if you two were to walk to Merripit House when we drew near that it would be less conspicuous should someone be close by. I'll be back here in 3 hours to pick you up."

The inspector quickly regained his composure. "'That's…that's true, of course. Mr. Holmes and I discussed that very subject last night. It…it must have slipped my mind. All right, sergeant, off we go now."

The two men exited the coach and began to head towards Merripit House while Perkins turned the carriage around and made his way back to Baskerville Hall. The sergeant looked to Lestrade as they walked side by side.

"Excuse me, inspector, but wouldn't it be better if we were to walk near the brush off the edge of the road to avoid detection?"

Lestrade blinked in surprise. "I…was about to offer up that very same suggestion. Good thinking, sergeant. After I solve this case, you will be mentioned in my report to Scotland Yard."

They walked beside the underbrush until they reached Merripit House. Bullfinch pulled a key from his pocket and placed it in the front door lock. The key turned effortlessly in the mechanism and he opened the door to a cold and silent interior.

"I'm glad I saved this house key from Mrs. Stapleton, inspector. I would feel strange breaking in, being an officer of the law and all."

"Another good idea, sergeant. You impress me very much. Look me up if you should wish to leave Grimpen and come to London. Now let's get cracking. You look around the first floor, and I'll take the second; and be sure to stay clear of the windows. After we search the premises, we'll keep watch hoping Stapleton decides to stop by, and then I'll have him."

They went their separate ways throughout the house, dodging windows and snooping about for signs that the baronet's cousin had visited there at some point. After a lengthy search, the two met at the bottom of the first floor staircase, each with an important piece of a puzzle.

"Well sergeant, did you discover anything of value?"

Bullfinch was eager to answer. "I may have, inspector. The pantry is completely empty; not a morsel of food left on the shelves."

Lestrade clapped his hands. "Aha! When I first arrived at the house to arrest Mrs. Stapleton, I allowed her to take a few articles of clothing but nothing else. No one was allowed to return here. Someone has been raiding this home for supplies or I'm a bloomin' duchess."

The sergeant was impressed. "Did YOU find any clues, inspector?"

"To be sure! Mrs. Stapleton's wardrobe has remained the way we left it, but most of her husband's clothes and some bedding materials are gone. Jack Stapleton has been here on more than one occasion; you can make book on it."

Bullfinch responded naively. "Then Mr. Holmes' theory about Mr. Stapleton still being alive, continuing in his quest to kill Sir Henry AND stealing from his own home were correct after all, right inspector?"

Lestrade's face burned with embarrassment, and he tried not to show his annoyance with his partner, but his words gave him away. "Yes, yes; the great Sherlock Holmes has begun to close in on his man once again. I've heard this song before, sergeant."

Now his face brightened. "But if we sit tight here in the house and Stapleton returns, this case will be solved by yours truly. Now I will go back upstairs and keep watch from the second floor; you do likewise here on the first, and be sure not to show yourself in any of the windows."

While the two policemen kept their silent vigil, Holmes and Watson were slowly walking the outside edge of the great Grimpen Mire. The doctor's face was glum as he dutifully followed in his friend's wake, both of them stopping occasionally to scan about the crags and marshes for some sign of a trail. Finally, he could take it no longer.

"You know that I am not a defeatist, Holmes, but I must admit to you that I feel this is a hopeless quest. The chance of us finding the path that Stapleton employs to enter and exit the mire is miniscule. This morass is miles in circumference. Holmes…are you even listening to what I'm saying?"

The great detective was closely examining a faded, tattered map; after a moment, he looked up. "Of course I'm listening, old chum, but we don't have to look for miles, at least for Stapleton's new residence. This map, which I obtained in the village, shows the exact location of the old abandoned tin mine where Stapleton kept his hound, and where he must presently reside today."

Watson grew more attentive. "Eureka! Then if we know where the mine is, we should be able to…"

Holmes unceremoniously cut him off. "Don't get yourself too worked up, Watson. The mine is in the very center of the mire. Stapleton could enter and exit from any direction."

The doctor's enthusiasm would not be deterred. "Perhaps there is someone in the village or hereabouts who still knows the way. It's worth a try."

Holmes was pleased that Watson had thought of the idea, but it was of little help. "I've already asked Mayor Sexton,

Reverend Musgrave, and Sergeant Bullfinch if they know of such a person. The mine closed many years ago. Anyone with such knowledge has either died or moved away. No Watson, our best bet is to find the path ourselves."

"But how can we? Stapleton pulled up the stakes that guided his way safely."

"He MUST be using some other means of identification that has eluded our scrutiny up to this point, something obvious to him but innocuous to us. Hello, we are coming up on the spot where Mr. Frankland met his untimely death. What is the name of that nearby rocky outcropping again, Watson?"

"Vixen Tor, Holmes; why?"

"Because I thought I detected some lingering smoke coming from around the back of it. Let's investigate, shall we, and do be quiet."

The two ventured cautiously to the base of the tor and waited for some sound or sign of movement. When none was forthcoming, they circled around the back of it and discovered the mouth of a small cave that had wisps of smoke arising from it. Watson drew his revolver as they began to creep inside and the light grew dim.

The doctor let out a whisper. "Careful Holmes; we don't know what we'll find in there. Perhaps this is the hideout of Stapleton's secret accomplice."

Holmes answered dejectedly when he reached the end of the tunnel. "It's empty, Watson. SOMEONE has been making use of this, but there's no sign of Stapleton. This is more likely the hovel of some moor tramp. These are absolutely primitive living conditions—goatskins for a bed, a single kettle over a dying fire, bones heaped in the corner. No one in their right mind would live here."

He leaned his back against the side of the cave wall and let out a long anguished sigh. "Watson, since the first time that we arrived here in Dartmoor, I have always been one step behind on the trail of Jack Stapleton. A number of innocent people have died because of this, and for all we know, Sir Henry could be next at any moment."

Watson tried to salve his friend's wounds. "Come, come, old boy; you are doing all that is humanly possible. The baronet has not fallen victim yet, and besides, he has that beast of a dog following him everywhere for added protection. Don't give up hope now."

Holmes smiled gratefully. "Thank you, Watson. If ever I needed cheering up, now is the time. Let us get back to Baskerville Hall. Sir Henry should be finishing up his walk of the grounds, and perhaps Lestrade has fared better on his end."

Watson's cheeks puffed outward for a moment in disgust. "I certainly hope NOT. I couldn't bear the thought of that pompous windbag besting us and solving this case. The man would be utterly insufferable in any future dealings with Scotland Yard and you know it."

Holmes laughed, and it felt good. "I daresay you're right Watson. Let us then hope...that SHADOW solves this case for us."

While Holmes and Watson started their trek back to Baskerville Hall, the squire and his dog were just finishing theirs. They had walked around the outer perimeter of the grounds several times, but always remained in sight of the hall. Sir Henry felt uncomfortable doing so, but followed Holmes' instructions to the letter. Nothing of any consequence or out of the ordinary had occurred, and neither man nor beast had seen a living soul. Now it was time to return to the warmth of the fireplace in the great room.

"What do you say, Shadow, shall we go back inside? I've walked about as much as I can; my bones are cold and I could use a stiff brandy by the fire. As for you...."

The squire looked down and stopped in mid-sentence. The dog had stiffened and leaned forward into a fighting stance. His hackles were up, and he gave out a low growl as he sniffed the air back and forth as though searching for the precise direction to expect the enemy. A faint wail was heard in the distance; Sir Henry shuddered, and the growl grew louder.

After a few moments, the sound was gone, and the dog relaxed, but the same could not be said of Sir Henry. "That's enough walking for one day, boy. That sound damned near made my blood run cold. Let's get back to the hall and see what dinner menu Mrs. Barrymore has planned for our guests; then it's off to Coombe Tracy to pick up Laura and go to Reverend Musgrave's big event."

CHAPTER 17

Murder And Abduction

A cold evening's rain fell on the sleepy village of Grimpen, but that could not erase the smile on Reverend Musgrave's face. This was his favorite event of the year. Most of the residents had already seated themselves inside the parish hall and were anxiously awaiting the start of the Jumble Sale.

It was a function that not only helped replenish the church coffers, but also provided parishioners an opportunity to purchase quality goods at an affordable price. All items were donated, many from individuals, and others from area merchants. But no one provided more than the squire from Baskerville Hall.

There was definitely an auction type of atmosphere; objects were placed conveniently on the stage for people to inspect before the bidding process went into full swing. When the general chatter began to subside, the reverend raised his hands.

"All right…all right…may I have everyone's attention? Before we kick off our annual sale, I would like to give special thanks to Sir Henry Baskerville, who was so VERY generous with his donations of clothing, furniture, and used silverware. I'm sure that I speak for all when I say that this year's items are the best we've ever exhibited for sale, and it is in large part due to his efforts."

A spontaneous round of applause erupted from the crowd. Sir Henry, seated in the front row next to Laura, Holmes, and Watson, got up and turned to the throng, smiling and bowing slightly in response. He had made a great impression on the populace with his previous plans for the region's infrastructure, and this only enhanced his standing in their eyes.

Musgrave decided to seize the moment. "Ladies and gentleman, I would like to take this opportunity to share some wonderful news with you. It is my honor to announce the bands of holy matrimony between Sir Henry Baskerville and Miss Laura Frankland. They plan to be married a month's time hence in our very own church, and ALL are invited to attend the ceremony and subsequent reception at Baskerville Hall."

The reverend walked quickly over to the baronet and shook his hand vigorously, and then exchanged a few pleasant words with Laura. "And may I say that I believe no one is more worthy of happiness than the two of you. Come on, everyone; three cheers for the squire and his fiancé."

The audience hesitated for one brief moment, but then took the cue. "HIP HIP...HORRAY! HIP HIP...HOORAY! HIP HIP...HOORAAAAY!"

Hats flew into the air and landed everywhere. Sir Henry motioned Laura to stand up. At first, she was embarrassed to do so, her being a newly divorced woman, but with the gentle urging of the reverend, she rose and waved meekly to the crowd with tears flowing down her cheeks.

All were pleased with the announcement; all but one, and he quickly exited the back of the hall without notice. An old man who had gone out to check on the weather for the walk home passed him in the dark.

"Where are you going in such a hurry, Murphy? Will you not bid on any of the items tonight?"

The gypsy was lost in thought, so he was startled by the question from the darkness. "Who is it? Oh, it's you, Bob Berry. No, there is nothing in there that I need, so it's off to bed. I have some...ah...horse trading to do early in the morning."

The old man gave him a sideward glance and stood in his way. "I'm sure. You have been out on the moor quite often in recent days. I could not help but notice as my home is on the outskirts of the village.

And it appears to me that you do most of your business at night, Murphy. Just what is it that you do out on the moor? Tell me, or I shall be forced to speak to Sergeant Bullfinch. He is not fond of gypsies, you know. He says that they are all thieves and troublemakers."

Murphy's face began to redden in anger, but it went unnoticed. Instead, he feigned a smile and spoke with a soothing voice. "Ha! I knew that I could not put anything past you. But if I tell you, do you promise not to tell a living soul? I will make it worth your while, believe me."

Berry swallowed the bait. "My farm has not prospered these past few years, and I am falling into debt. Are we talking about money? That would go a long way in ensuring my silence."

Murphy nodded. "Absolutely; I am talking about GOLD!"

Berry scoffed. "What kind of fool do you take me for? There is no gold on the moor, Murphy. The only metal of any use out there was tin from the old mine, and that vein thinned out a long time ago."

"Not gold from the ground, Bob; gold hidden and left behind by the Romans who conquered England and this area in particular from centuries past. I have found Roman coins in a cave not an hour's drive from here. Would you like to search for some yourself? I can take you there."

The farmer nearly squealed in delight. "YES...YES I WOULD. But must we go now? It is late, and how will we see in the dark?"

"No need to worry about that. I have torches fixed to the walls of the cave. All we need do is light them once we enter. Besides, if we go in the daytime, we might be spotted. The fewer who roam about this location, the better for us, don't you agree...partner?"

Now it was Berry who smiled. "I certainly do. I saw your cart around the side of the hall before it got dark. Let us be off then."

The old man chattered away with excitement as the cart wound its way slowly out onto the moor. The rain meant nothing to him now. On the other hand, Murphy was mostly silent. Finally, they reached the base of Vixen Tor, and Nicola brought the cart to a halt.

"This is our destination Bob. Get a torch from the back, but don't try to light it until we get inside the mouth of the cave. Someone may see the glow in the distance."

Berry was quick to agree. "Of course, of course; we must be careful."

The pair gradually found their way to the back of the tor and its entrance. Murphy held back a few paces, allowing Berry to get ahead of him.

"All right; light the torch Bob, and go in slowly."

Berry did so with a flick of a match against the rock wall. The flame lit their way for only a few paces. "Where are the rest of those torches on the walls you spoke of? We need more light than this."

Murphy rubbed the talisman around his neck and was stepping backwards out of the cave when he answered. "Just a few yards more and you will find what you're looking for...you meddlesome old fool."

Before Berry could answer, the torch was ripped from his hand. A piercing scream ensued, followed by the cackling of insane laughter. Murphy ran to his cart and made a hasty retreat for the Grimpen Mire and the general location of the hidden pathway that led to the mine. The rain finally stopped. He lit a candle and waved it back and forth until it was answered by another spec of light; then he snuffed out the flame with his fingers and waited in the darkness.

The added dampness from the showers gave the moor and mire a dank odor that permeated the air. There was no escaping the smell. In about 10 minute's time, Murphy heard the slogging of footsteps coming towards him. There was no doubt in his mind who was approaching.

Stapleton was curious. "This meeting was not previously agreed to. You're fortunate that I was out taking a short walk and I saw the light. What is so important?"

"We must talk, Jack. I was at the village Jumble Sale earlier this evening, and Reverend Musgrave announced the impending marriage of Sir Henry to Laura Lyons. It shall happen within a month's time, I believe."

The news was not well received. "Leave it to my cousin to thicken the soup. No matter, that only means that we shall have to kill BOTH of them, but it must happen soon."

Murphy was not finished with his news. "While I was in the hall, I also overheard Reverend Musgrave talking to Mayor Sexton. It seems that Sir Henry must go to London tomorrow to sign some important business papers for his solicitors. He will take the early train out of Oakhampton and not return until later in the evening. I'm sure that someone will accompany him on the journey after what happened the last time, don't you think?"

His partner agreed. "I have no doubt. That leaves one person to manage things back here; that is in our favor."

"But what about Sergeant Bullfinch and the London inspectc ?"

Stapleton laughed. "Those two dolts are busy watching Merripit House, but that henhouse has been picked clean; they are too late on that score."

Murphy grew anxious. "So what IS our plan then, Jack?"

"It is actually quite simple. Tomorrow night, as soon as the sun goes down, use your wonderful powers of persuasion and bring Laura Lyons to Vixen Tor. We will be waiting for you both."

Murphy was confused. "Then what, Jack?"

"Then we will spring the trap that lures my cousin to Vixen Tor, and his death. Wait a moment."

Stapleton went back inside the mine and returned a few minutes later with a small sheet of writing paper with a message printed on it. He handed it to Murphy. The gypsy read its contents but was still unsure. He was also displeased.

"How do I get this to Baskerville Hall at the right time while also remaining undetected? That won't be an easy task."

"Oh, but it will. Before you head to Coombe Tracey to kidnap Laura, ride over to Princetown. Because of the prison nearby, the village boasts an excellent post office. No one there knows you. Give explicit instructions that this letter must be delivered to Sir Henry at precisely 6PM that evening, and make sure that you inform the clerks that you will pay double the fee for this special service. Nothing gets the attention of a civil servant more than money."

Murphy was relieved, but still irritated. "That's fine by me. But why can't we simply kill them ourselves? Why must the plan include Vixiana?"

Jack grew angry. "Because I wish to see him die slowly in the most excruciating and horrifying way possible. I've waited far too long to obtain what is rightfully mine, and living like an animal has only increased my hatred.

And get that damned witch out of your head once and for all. When she has performed her task, I will keep the bargain and set her free. Besides, I have no desire to curry disfavor with such a creature, whether I am in Dartmoor or Costa Rica."

"It looks as though you have thought of everything, Jack," Murphy admitted. "But is this just about the inheritance?"

Stapleton beamed with approval. "Ha, so you sense that there is more to this, ay Nicola? Well, you would be correct. That damned Sherlock Holmes foiled my plans once before, and it very nearly cost me my life. After we have succeeded, the world will see that I gave him a merry chase until I finally murdered my cousin under his very nose…and he will not be able to prove it."

Back in Grimpen, the Jumble Sale had ended, and everyone was saying their good nights, including the squire. "Why the sad face, Laura? I'll only be gone for most of the day tomorrow. Dr. Watson and I will leave on the 6:00AM train out of Oakhampton and be back at the hall by dusk. That's not so bad."

Laura was surprised. "Dr. Watson is going with you? Why not Mr. Holmes? I appreciate all of the doctor's efforts on our behalf, but he seems a bit of a bumbler, to put it kindly."

Sir Henry tried to suppress a chuckle, but failed. "I know what you mean, Laura, but Holmes told me that Watson has stood by him in many a tight corner. He will be of great service.

Besides, Holmes said that he had some investigating to do in the village that could not wait. I asked the good doctor what it was, and he was very put out about it. It seems that Mr. Holmes does not like to divulge any fresh theories until he has tested them first, and that includes his close friend Watson."

The squire bent down and kissed her hand. "Now allow Perkins to take you home, and I shall wait here for his return. Don't worry." Laura heeded the request, and he watched the carriage ride out of sight toward Coombe Tracey.

Holmes was close by. "So, Sir Henry, are you all set for your brief sojourn tomorrow?"

"Yes, Mr. Holmes, but Laura secretly told me that her intuition leads her to believe this mystery will be coming to a swift conclusion."

The detective raised an eyebrow. "Is that so? Very interesting...to tell the truth, I feel the same way."

The night passed without incident, but Shadow was restless. The dog paced back and forth by a first floor window, occasionally staring out into the gloom as though on guard. Before dawn, the Barrymores crept down the front stairs carrying several suitcases. They passed through the foyer and were about to exit the hall when Eliza spied a pair of red eyes fixed upon them through the dim light. She suppressed a shriek but froze in her tracks, dropping her belongings. Her husband walked slowly to the door and opened it.

"Don't look at it, Eliza. Gently come towards me; just put one foot in front of the other. I know you can do this."

She whispered back as though hoping the dog would not hear. "I have never seen eyes shine that color from a dog before, and I have been around them all my life. It's not natural."

Under the circumstances, Barrymore thought it best not to dispute her opinion. In truth, he agreed with her, but it was imperative that he showed no fear to either of them. He spoke soothingly to her.

"A few more paces and you are out...that's it...just a bit further...there you are. Now take my bags outside and wait for me while I go back for yours."

Eliza breathed a sigh of relief when she stepped out of the house. Barrymore summoned his courage and made for the bags on the floor. His peripheral vision could see the red eyes continuing to stare at him, never even bothering to blink. The hair on the back of his neck stood up.

He grasped the belongings unhurriedly and focused his concentration on the open door. In a few moments, he was outside, quietly closing the door behind them. It was only then that they could both relax and take a deep breath. As they walked away, Eliza admitted her shame.

"I know that this is in our best interests, but we are deserting Sir Henry in his hour of need."

Barrymore was more practical. "We are saving our LIVES. My family served in that house for generations, where many Baskervilles met sad and mysterious fates. I will not be touched by it any longer. We loved Sir Charles and he is dead. If Holmes cannot protect the new squire, then we should get far away from here. Let us speak no more of it."

The next day, despite the obvious signs of his servants stealthy departure during the night, Sir Henry and Watson left as scheduled. Legal entanglements in London left no other choice. The baronet was surprised and slightly unnerved by their desertion, so Lestrade and Sergeant Bullfinch were instructed by Holmes to remain and keep watch over the hall and grounds while he was to be driven to the village on his latest fact finding mission.

Later, as Perkins guided the carriage towards Grimpen, a lone rider on horseback passed him on the road. There was no thought to give the man any scrutiny, as Nicola Murphy was a familiar face on Dartmoor. The gypsy surmised that an adversary was in the coach, but he could not see who it was.

This was all he better for him, for if he had known that Sherlock Holmes was the passenger, he might have abandoned his mission. But he did not, and within 2 hours hard ride the bleak and foreboding hilltop prison of Princetown was in full view. The town was nestled in a nearby valley, and although quaint and peaceful, the image of the penitentiary permanently loomed over it like an evil vision.

The events unfolded just as Stapleton had said they would. No one in Princetown gave Murphy as much as a second look. He strode confidently into the municipal post office and outlined his needs for the delivery of the letter. When the clerk balked and said it was doubtful that such a precise timetable could be accomplished on such short notice, Murphy promptly handed over double the amount, abruptly settling the issue.

One third of Stapleton's instructions for this important day had been accomplished. There was still much to be done, but Murphy knew that he had time to undertake an additional task, and he made straight for the moor for a meeting with Syeira. This would be his last chance to convince her that taming the witch could be done safely, and for the betterment of their people.

But that conversation would never take place. As he rode passed the outer wagons, women were wailing and pulling their hair, men were cursing, and the camp dogs were whimpering in fear. When Murphy reached the encampment, he spied Syeira in the center of it all being pelted with stones and tree limbs.

She was a bloody pulp, barely alive. The sound of his approaching horse turned the gypsies' attention towards him. Murphy screamed at them to stop, and that they did, but not because of his command. He was now in grave danger.

"WHY ARE YOU DOING THIS TO MY GRANDMOTHER? WHAT HAS SHE DONE TO DESERVE SUCH TREATMENT FROM HER OWN KIND?"

The answer was quick and to the point. It was from Fredor, a family elder. "Nadya and Yanko, the twelve year old twins of Maria Oospenskyia, went out before dusk last night to search for herbs and flowers. They never returned. During the night, the camp dogs began to howl, then they drew to the center of the camp whimpering and fearful of leaving the safety of the fire."

He moved closer to Murphy's horse, eyeing the bridle. "We know that she performed some evil magic for you. THIS is the direct result. She must be punished, and now that you are here, YOU shall join her in death."

Fredor made a grab for the leather straps, but Murphy was too quick for him. A quick jerk of the bridle turned the horse towards the direction of the road and safety. He dug his heels into the horse's flanks and it reared up and galloped off. He never looked back. The image of his grandmother's body was etched in his memory, and it was at that moment he was pledged completely to Stapleton's plan.

Now the baronet had a second mortal enemy. In Nicola's twisted logic, it was Sir Henry's fault that his grandmother suffered such an ignominious death. He followed the road towards Grimpen and switched his conveyance to the horse and cart, then headed obediently to Coombe Tracey. He stopped to have a light meal at the local pub and waited patiently at a table in a back corner until dusk had thoroughly settled in.

Under the cover of darkness, Murphy pulled up in front of the flat that belonged to Laura Lyons. There was no one out or about. He strode briskly up the path and rapped quietly on her front door. He waited, and then did it a second time. He heard rustling and the sound of approaching footsteps. Laura opened the door and innocently asked. "Good evening. May I help you, sir?"

Murphy leered at her in controlled anger and stepped forward. "Oh yes...yes you can."

CHAPTER 18

End Game

It was an unenthusiastic group of guests that sat glumly at the dining room table of Baskerville Hall. They were just finishing an early cold supper of yesterday's mutton and potatoes, courtesy of Eliza Barrymore's last prepared meal. Watson slowly picked at the meat with his fork and finally gave up with a sigh. Lestrade, so used to eating whatever and whenever he could when on duty, put on a game face and made a valiant effort to clear half his plate.

Holmes, as usual, barely touched his food. He passed his time going over some written notes at the far end of the table, while Perkins and the chamber maid April began to take away the dishes. Sir Henry stood up and spoke to his companions with great humility.

"My friends, I know that you deserved a better meal than this, but it was the best that I could do under the circumstances. I have spoken with Reverend Musgrave and he has graciously offered the services of his cook and housekeeper, Mrs. Beale until I can make arrangements to fill the positions previously held by the Barrymores. She will arrive tomorrow morning, and I am told that…"

There was a loud knock at the front door. Holmes got up, walked to the window, and looked out. A postman holding a letter stood waiting for the door to open. Holmes glanced over at the grandfather clock in the hallway.

"That is odd…a postman delivering a letter at 6PM in the evening. I suppose someone should accept the communication."

Sir Henry volunteered. "It must be from my solicitors in London with more legal papers. If you would excuse me, gentlemen. I shall only be a moment."

The squire left the room and opened the front door. The young man who was waiting outside tried to make the most of his moment, but failed miserably by mistaking the baronet for the butler. He straightened up and cleared his throat before speaking.

"I haves a letter here for one Sir Henry Baskerville. It was to be delivered to him personally no later than 6PM, and 6PM it is. Would you be so kind as to fetch him for me? It must be important."

The squire smiled and handed the lad a pound note. "I am Sir Henry. Thank you for your trouble."

The lad blinked in shock for a brief moment, but recovered quickly when he focused on his generous tip and bounded off to his cart. The squire opened the envelope with mild interest, but that emotion turned to abject fear when he read its contents:

Henry Baskerville,

If you wish to see your fiancé live beyond this night, then come ALONE to Vixen Tor just off the main road, near the spot where old man Frankland met his end. If you tell anyone about the contents of this letter, she dies. If anyone accompanies you, she dies. If you do not come to the Tor tonight, she dies.

He stared at the letter for several seconds, his mind swirling with thoughts that he could not control. The sound of laughter from the dining hall brought him back to reality. He knew full well this was a trap to lure him away from his guardians, but there was nothing else that he could do…other than obey.

This would require a command performance. Taking a long, deep breath, he placed the letter in his shirt pocket and re-entered the dining hall. His appearance was calm and collected.

"Gentlemen, the correspondence was indeed from my solicitors. If you would excuse me for a moment, I must look over some papers in my room and be ready to respond to them in the morning."

Holmes responded casually. "Of course, Sir Henry. When you return, I shall go over an interesting observation with all of you that I made whilst out on the moor."

The squire made his way up to the second floor, stood at the top of the stairs for a moment, and then went straight to Watson's room. As he opened the door and stepped inside, he felt a presence. Whirling around, there was Shadow following in his wake. The dog appeared uneasy. Sir Henry patted him on the head and spoke quietly.

"I know, good boy. You sense that something is wrong. Well…you're correct, but I can't take you with me, as much as I'd like to."

He went over to the nightstand, picked up Watson's service revolver, and put it in his pocket. The squire gave one final look at the letter and deliberately placed it in the middle of the bed. That was all he could do under the circumstances. Leaving the room, he stole down the servants stairs into the kitchen and out the back door. Shadow stood watching and whined quietly as his master walked briskly towards the main road and his uncertain future.

Out on the moor, Vixiana stood atop her tor and peered anxiously into the darkness for her quarry to arrive. With the baronet's death, she would be finally freed from her servitude. Inside the cave, impatience was the virtue as Stapleton and Murphy continued to get in each other's way as they paced back and forth with anticipation. The pleading eyes of a helpless, bound and gagged Laura meant absolutely nothing to them.

Stapleton broke the silence. "Nicola, go out and check up on your witch. I don't want her to do anything stupid this late in the game. And stay there to make certain that Sir Henry has not brought along any unexpected guests."

He peeked at Laura with an evil smile and went towards her. "However, I doubt that he would have the nerve; that would bring about your immediate death, wouldn't it my dear? I wonder if he realizes that you will die regardless."

Laura turned away and began to sob quietly as Murphy followed his instructions and left the cave. Besides the amulet he received from Syeira, he had his own revolver in hand. This made him feel safe from harm.

He called up to the witch in a hushed tone. "Do you see anyone yet? You must be ready to strike at a moment's notice."

Her laughing reply chilled him. "I see no one, but I can sometimes smell a Baskerville approaching; have no fear. Long have I waited to thank the heirs of Sir Hugo for their ill treatment of me after his death. Only HE was able to understand and truly appreciate my greatness. This will be a sweet slaying."

Murphy responded carefully. "Remember, Vixiana, my master wishes to watch him die. Do not spoil the plan. Fulfill your part of the bargain, and he will do likewise." There was no verbal reply, and the inane cackling did not give him reassurance.

Back at Baskerville Hall, Lestrade was growing impatient as he watched Holmes brush a small stone in his hands. "Come,

come, Mr. Holmes; what's this interesting observation that you are so keen to tell us about?"

Watson replied for his partner. "If you must know, he's waiting for Sir Henry to return. Now that you mention it, the squire HAS been gone for some time now. I think I'll go up and see what's keeping him."

The doctor climbed the stairs; there at the top lay Shadow with sad eyes watching him as he went by. Watson went to the master bedroom and knocked respectfully on the closed door. When there was no answer, he cleared his throat and spoke up.

"Hello, Sir Henry? It's Dr. Watson. Are you nearly finished with your paperwork? Holmes would like everyone together so he can reveal some fact or other."

There was no answer. Watson opened the door and became uneasy when he could not locate the baronet. As he was on his way back to tell the others of the disappearance, he noticed that his own door was open, and he remembered closing it earlier in the day. Walking inside the bedroom, the first thing he noticed, or rather did not notice, was his service revolver.

He opened the nightstand drawer hoping he had placed it there, but that was a false hope. He glanced inadvertently at his bed and there was the letter left by Sir Henry. The doctor picked it up and read it with horror. Downstairs, the detectives heard a cry ring out.

"HOLMES, HOLMES, we have been bested again!" They jumped from their chairs and ran to the hallway just as Watson and Shadow reached the bottom of the stairs.

Lestrade was almost frantic. "What is it, doctor? What's gone wrong?"

Watson handed the note to the Scotland Yarder; he read and passed it quickly to Holmes, who crumpled it in his hands in marked irritation and then looked up to speak.

"Gentlemen, we haven't a moment to lose. Sir Henry has had a head start on us that will most certainly result in his death. That fiend Stapleton! I will run to the squire's aid until my heart bursts if that's what it takes."

As they hurried out the front door to the main road, Watson offered some hope. "Holmes, Sir Henry took my service revolver with him; that means the squire's still has a fighting chance if he can just sniff out that rascal before any harm comes to Laura."

Holmes stopped dead in his tracks and very nearly screamed with joy. "WATSON, YOU"VE GOT IT! Sniff him out you said, ay? Well, Shadow can get there much faster, and without drawing undue attention."

Holmes ran back inside the hall, retrieved the letter and placed it under the dog's nose. "All right, Shadow; your master is in serious trouble. Find him NOW!"

The dog took to the road as though on command and darted off into the dark night. The trio followed in his wake as quickly as they could. Watson began to fall behind the others, but not before he voiced a macabre irony.

"Think of it, gentlemen. Over 300 years ago, a savage dog hunted down Sir Hugo Baskerville and tore him to shreds. Now, another Baskerville is being chased in just the same manner, but this dog is trying to SAVE his life."

Holmes was now far ahead but he heard his partner's remark. "The irony has not escaped me, Watson. We can only hope that Shadow gets there in time to offer Sir Henry some assistance until we arrive."

Meanwhile, Murphy stood at the base of the tor and checked his pistol. The five shots in the cylinder would be more than enough if something went wrong. The firearm gave him a sense of security, and he held it tight. Vixiana remained perched above him, rocking back and forth in anticipation of the kill. She did not have long to wait.

Sir Henry's outline began to appear out of the gloom striding swiftly towards them. Vixiana spied him approaching and turned round and round with her arms outstretched. A thick fog arose from the moor, quickly enveloping the area, but not before Sir Henry recognized the spot where Laura's father had died.

As the mist thickened, he crouched down and placed his hand along the ground in an effort to feel the roadbed beneath him. He knew it was vital that he remain on firm footing if he was to save Laura and himself. When he calculated that he was closing in on the tor, he stood up and waited. Now it would be a game of nerves.

Murphy was the first to crack under the pressure. After several minutes, he whispered up to Vixiana. "Why doesn't he step into the bog, or at least call out to us? He MUST know that we are here."

The witch answered thoughtfully. "This Baskerville is cunning…not to be underestimated. I will call out and distract him while you venture forth and capture him for my pleasure. Helloooo stranger. I am a crippled old gypsy lost in the night fog. Will you not come forward and help me back to my camp? You will be rewarded by my people, I promise you."

No reply was forthcoming. Murphy cursed under his breath; he had had enough. He cocked his pistol and stepped into the mist, eventually disappearing from Vixiana's view. In a few short moments, a shot rang out, alerting Stapleton inside the cave that something had gone terribly wrong.

Vixiana peered anxiously into the fog, expecting to see Murphy appear triumphant. What she beheld was absolutely appalling. At first, she spied two blazing red eyes rushed toward her. As they got closer, the form of an immense hound materialized and charged up the tor snarling with a sound that could only indicate a fight to the death.

There would be no time for her to react. The hound leaped into the air and both of them toppled over the top of the tor and into the neighboring bog that had been meant for the squire. Sir Henry could be heard yelling frantically in the mist. "SHADOW...SHADOW...WAIT FOR ME!"

But it was too late. Witch and hound were locked in a death struggle as the bog slowly sucked them down. Vixiana made one attempt to break free and reach the safety of the road, but Shadow locked onto her thigh and dragged her backwards.

The mist dissipated, and Holmes and Lestrade could be seen in the background running towards the fray, with Watson not far behind. Vixiana knew that her cause was hopeless. Even as Shadow disappeared beneath the muck, he held onto his quarry, as evidenced by her form continuing to be jerked under the mire.

Finally, she uttered her last words before slipping under. "THE HOUND! THE HOUND OF HELL! OH DAMNED CREATURE! CAVE CANEM NOCTEEEEE!"

In a moment, all was quiet. The trio reached Sir Henry just as Murphy's horse cart raced passed them with a furious Stapleton at the reigns. It was all they could do to get out of the way. The squire ran to the back of the tor and entered the cave. There was Laura, still bound and gagged, but alive. The baronet untied her bonds and hugged her tightly.

"My sweet dear, I thought that I had lost you. Are you hurt?"

Laura responded breathlessly. "Oh, Henry; it was horrible. I was to be cast into the bog after you. How could people be so evil? I was in a nightmare but could not wake up, and then I heard a shot."

"I am unharmed. It was Murphy whom I killed in the fog, and just at the last moment, I have to admit. He was taking aim at me when Shadow ran past and distracted him just long enough for me to shoot first...OH MY GOD! SHADOW!"

They hurried out and found Inspector Lestrade standing near the bog, looking down. "I am truly sorry, Sir Henry. By the time we got close enough, the dog and that old woman had both gone under. There was nothing we could do."

The squire looked around with a confused look on his face. "Where…where are Mr. Holmes and Dr. Watson?"

Lestrade pointed back the way they came. The two were running as fast as their legs would carry them. When they reached a fork in the road, Holmes pointed to the right. "This way, Watson."

The doctor was not so self-assured. "How can you be so certain Holmes?"

"Stapleton is evidently attempting to return to the safety of the tin mine, where he feels he will be invulnerable."

Watson grew alarmed. "But Holmes, if that scoundrel should get back safely inside the Grimpen Mire, we may never find him. He has all of those supplies from Merripit House, and…look Holmes, there's the cart, and it appears to be abandoned."

Murphy's horse cart was just around a short bend in the road. Stapleton had evidently decided to continue on foot. The doctor was nearly inconsolable.

"I knew it, Holmes. My God…lost him again. We've failed Sir Henry once more. Will he ever be safe?"

Holmes stared into the mire with a smile. "I seriously doubt that Stapleton will escape his judgment THIS time, Watson. I do not believe he will reach that mine alive."

Watson was confused. "But I don't understand Holmes. The man knows the mire like the back of his hand. What makes things so different now?"

Holmes waited patiently for his friend to pause. "Watson, do you remember back when we foiled Stapleton's plot the first time, he pulled up his markers so he that could not be followed to the mine?"

"Why, yes, of course, but how he has been able to accomplish that task afterwards has been the real mystery."

"Ah, a mystery that I may have solved. The other day while walking about the moor on my own, I noticed several rocks of bluish black color along the outer perimeter of this very spot heading into the mire. There is one right over there.

I chipped a piece from the first stone and took it into town for analysis. It seems that it is called quarry granite. To the casual observer, it's just another rock scattered about the mire. The essential minerals are 30% quartz, 60% feldspar, and 10% mica. What makes it interesting is that THIS type of stone is only found when one digs deep in the earth, or as in this case, our tin mine."

Watson's face began to brighten and he listened attentively. "So I took a calculated risk and followed the supposed markers into the mire, and then switched the locations of several of them further in. If my hypothesis is correct, then..."

Just at that moment, a blood curdling cry rang out. It was Stapleton. "OH MY GOD. SOMEONE HELP ME PLEASE! I AM GOING UNDER. CAN ANYONE HEAR ME? I AM SINKIN...."

The scream stopped suddenly, and all was silent. Holmes put a hand on the shoulder of his friend. "I can now state definitively that Sir Henry Baskerville has no further need of our services, Watson."

Epilogue

Acold rain silently pelted Mrs. Hudson's boarding house. Watson brushed the curtains aside and glanced out the window to the street below. Just as he was about to look away a ragged young newsboy raced up the sidewalk and rang the doorbell. The doctor heard a subdued conversation, which concluded with Mrs. Hudson scolding the boy for dripping on her oval rug, and then the swift sound of footsteps on the second floor stairs. Rather than wait for the inevitable knock, he hastily opened the door.

The boy was drenched, but he proudly held out a dry copy of the London Times for inspection. Watson observed it carefully without a word, then reached into his pocket and gave the lad a coin. The amount was not what he had hoped for, but on the other hand, it did not come as a surprise, either. With a tip of his cap he raced down the stairs and into the bleak November weather.

Watson wobbled over to his favorite chair, sat down and began to thumb through the pages for news. In a few minutes he came upon an article that caught his attention, and he was most anxious to share it with his roommate.

"Holmes, I've just read here that Sir Henry Baskerville and Laura Frankland were married a few days ago at the local church in Grimpen, which was followed by a huge reception at Baskerville Hall. I'm so glad for them...especially Laura. The poor girl had quite a stretch of bad luck, but now, her future is bright, and I daresay that Sir Henry will be a devoted husband. What do you think of that?"

There was no reply to the doctor's question. He put the paper down and peeked over at his friend standing upright in front of the fireplace with his arms folded, staring at the dying fire. The doctor grew concerned.

"Dash it all Holmes, what is it? You've been moping around here for weeks, ever since we returned from Dartmoor; and you've hardly uttered a word today. How can you NOT be happy? The case is finally closed, Sir Henry is safe, and Stapleton has received his long overdue just reward."

Holmes sighed and turned to his old friend. "I'm sorry that I haven't been better company lately Watson. It's just that…I thought in this one instance…after all these years of searching…we might finally uncover tangible proof of the supernatural."

Watson stared at him in total disbelief. "How can you possibly say such things, Holmes? What about the hound, and the witch? How much more proof do you NEED for heaven's sake?"

He replied with considerable bitterness. "Much more than I've been shown, I'm afraid."

Watson grew irritated. "Then how do you explain what happened on the moor that frightful night?"

Holmes shook his head. "It's very simple. Shadow, who you believe was the legendary Hound of the Baskervilles, was nothing more than a wild moor dog tamed by an act of kindness that it never had experienced before in its life. I will grant you that he was unusually large, but that should not imply that Shadow was in any way supernatural."

Watson's mouth dropped in disbelief. "Well then, what about that horrible witch? You saw her for yourself. Laura said that Stapleton told her how Murphy dredged her up from the muck after hundreds of years, how she was the evil Vixiana that the tor was actually named after."

"I'll wager that under the circumstances, Stapleton would have told Laura anything to keep her at bay until Sir Henry's arrival, Watson. The woman was nothing more than a crazy old moor gypsy discovered by Murphy, Stapleton's well hidden accomplice."

The doctor began to sputter. "But you heard the witch scream before she died, Holmes; she shouted "Cave Canem Nocte." That's the very Latin inscription inscribed on the Baskerville crest. You saw it for yourself many times; it's painted on the carriage door. The literal translation is Beware the Dog of Night. That old witch KNEW of the hound's existence from hundreds of years ago, Holmes."

There was only silence. Soon Watson's tone and manner changed to one of sympathy and support, as he finally realized the intense inner turmoil that his friend had been experiencing since their return.

"Holmes…the supernatural does not announce itself on a billboard. Sometimes one must interpret events from a different perspective and simply take things…on faith." The great detective lowered his head and stared into the fire.

Author's Notes

I know what you're going to ask. The question is...am I
crazy? Sir Arthur Conan Doyle is an acclaimed writer loved
my millions. His principal character, Sherlock Holmes, is
arguably the most well-known fictional character in the world.
Finally, "The Hound of the Baskervilles" is his most famous and
popular story.

Why then would I leave myself open to the many slings and
arrows of outrageous fortune by taking up where Doyle left off
at the conclusion of his Hound and create an ongoing storyline
and alternate ending? The answer is simple. I love "Hound of
the Baskervilles." It is my personal favorite fiction story, (followed closely by Washington Irving's "Legend of Sleepy Hollow)."

However, as many times as I've read the book and watched
the movies made as a result of it, I still can't help but be dissatisfied by the way the story played out; that is, in the end, there
never really was a hound from hell. And I may be going out on
a limb, but I think many readers were also disappointed,
although they would never come out and say so.

"Hound of the Baskervilles" was not written any better
than the many other Holmes stories, but it contained the possible supernatural element that kept people on edge from
chapter to chapter; and ultimately, when Doyle did not pro-

duce that element, that's where I believe he stumbled ever so slightly, (in my humble opinion).

If he had actually created a hound from hell, I believe his reading public would have stood up and cheered. Remember, Doyle wrote at a time when spiritualism was all the rage in England, and he was a firm believer himself. Because of this, I always found it odd that he ended the Hound story the way he did.

As for the characters in MY story, I patterned them after the Universal Sherlock Holmes movies cast members; that is, Basil Rathbone as Holmes, Nigel Bruce as Watson, Dennis Hoey as Lestrade, and Mary Gordon as Mrs. Hudson. I realize that the Watson in the Universal films in no way resembles the Watson in Doyle's tales, but I watched the movies too many times not to have those images seared into my mind.

A fan of those Universal flics may well have recognized some familiar names in my story—Sexton, Musgrave, Bullfinch and Bleeker to name a few, along with a fair number of quotes. It is my homage to those wonderful films that allowed me to escape inside them and enjoy every minute, even though I always knew the endings.

I also did not forget the very well done Hammer Studios color version of "Hound of the Baskervilles," with Peter Cushing as Holmes and Andre Morell as Watson. As in all of the Hammer films, great musical background mood music was especially appealing. I tried to include a few elements from that movie also.

Finally, there is the two part BBC television version of Hound of the Baskervilles, again starring Peter Cushing as Holmes, with Nigel Stock as Watson. At the beginning of this particular film, the Baskerville crest is shown within a stained glass window at the hall, and under the crest there is the Latin inscription Cave Canem Nocte—Beware the Dog of Night. I was very happy to be able to pluck that golden nugget and place it in my story. This BBC effort is not particularly well known but worth checking out by all Hound aficionados.

In summation, I hope that Sherlock Holmes fans will enjoy this new twist to the story and also its alternative ending. I would also like to thank my poor wife Karen, who has had to edit every chapter of my books and to Bob Berry for creating such a great cover.

CPSIA information can be obtained at www.ICGtesting.com
Printed in the USA
BVOW05s1117250115

384830BV00001B/54/P